14

An invitation to investiga
and the ideas that inhabit the
OTHER WORLDS OF CLIFFORD SIMAK

DUSTY ZEBRA:
Trader loved all the little zebras he received in return for his miraculous cleaning gadgets. But then, all that accumulated dust had to be deposited SOMEwhere.

CARBON COPY:
Everybody was happy with the handsome new housing development until the alien practical joker perpetrated one joke too many.

FOUNDING FATHER:
Self-delusion is a helpful drug— in small doses.

IDIOT'S CRUSADE:
Which turned out not to be so idiotic after all.

DEATH SCENE:
Clairvoyance can prevent wars—could it also deaden the excitement of living?

GREEN THUMB:
Which won't surprise people who have one and should be included in every gardening manual.

OTHER WORLDS of

CLIFFORD SIMAK

(Six stories from the original edition titled "The Worlds of Clifford Simak")

CLIFFORD SIMAK

AVON BOOK DIVISION
The Hearst Corporation
572 Madison Avenue—New York 22, N.Y.

Acknowledgement is hereby made to the following magazines in which these stories first appeared: *Galaxy Magazine*—"Dusty Zebra," "Carbon Copy," "Founding Father," "Idiot's Crusade," "Green Thumb." *Infinity Science Fiction*—"Death Scene."

Contents

Dusty Zebra

IF YOU'RE HUMAN, you can't keep a thing around the house. You're always losing things and never finding them and you go charging through the place, yelling, cross-examining, blaming.

That's the way it is in all families.

Just one warning—don't try to figure out where all those things have gone or who might have taken them. If you have any notion of investigating, forget it. You'll be happier!

I'll tell you how it was with me.

I'd bought the sheet of stamps on my way home from the office so I could mail out the checks for the monthly bills. But I'd just sat down to write the checks when Marge and Lewis Shaw dropped over. I don't care much for Lewis and he barely tolerates me. But Marge and Helen are good friends, and they got to talking, and the Shaws stayed all evening.

Lewis told me about the work he was doing at his research laboratory out at the edge of town. I tried to switch him off to something else, but he kept right on. I suppose he's so interested in his work that he figures everyone else must be. But I don't know a thing about electronics and I can't tell a microgauge from a microscope.

It was a fairly dismal evening and the worst of it was that I couldn't say so. Helen would have jumped all over me for being antisocial.

So, the next evening after dinner, I went into the den to write the checks and, of course, the stamps were gone.

I had left the sheet on top of the desk and now the desk

was bare except for one of the Bildo-Blocks that young Bill had outgrown several years before, but which still turn up every now and then in the most unlikely places.

I looked around the room. Just in case they might have blown off the desk, I got down on my hands and knees and searched under everything. There was no sign of the stamps.

I went into the living room, where Helen was curled up in a chair, watching television.

"I haven't seen them, Joe," she said. "They must be where you left them."

It was exactly the kind of answer I should have expected.

"Bill might know," I said.

"He's scarcely been in the house all day. When he does show up, you've got to speak to him."

"What's the matter now?"

"It's this trading business. He traded off that new belt we got him for a pair of spurs."

"I can't see anything wrong in that. When I was a kid . . ."

"It's not just the belt," she said. "He's traded everything. And the worst of it is that he always seems to get the best of it."

"The kid's smart."

"If you take that attitude, Joe . . ."

"It's not *my* attitude," I said. "It's the attitude of the whole business world. When Bill grows up . . ."

"When he grows up, he'll be in prison. Why, the way he trades, you'd swear he was training to be a con man!"

"All right, I'll talk to him."

I went back into the den because the atmosphere wasn't exactly as friendly as it might have been and, anyhow, I had to send out those checks, stamps or no stamps.

I got the pile of bills and the checkbook and the fountain pen out of the drawer. I reached out and picked up the Bildo-Block to put it to one side, so I'd have a good, clear space to work on. But the moment I picked it up, I knew that this thing was no Bildo-Block.

8

It was the right size and weight and was black and felt like plastic, except that it was slicker than any plastic I had ever felt. It felt as if it had oil on it, only it didn't.

I set it down in front of me and pulled the desk lamp closer. But there wasn't much to see. It still looked like one of the Bildo-Blocks.

Turning it around, I tried to make out what it was. On the second turn, I saw the faint oblong depression along one side of it—a very shallow depression, almost like a scratch.

I looked at it a little closer and could see that the depression was machined and that within it was a faint red line. I could have sworn the red line flickered just a little. I held it there, studying it, and could detect no further flicker. Either the red had faded or I had been seeing things to start with, for after a few seconds I couldn't be sure there was any line at all.

I figured it must have been something Bill had picked up or traded for. The kid is more than half pack-rat, but there's nothing wrong with that, nor with the trading, either, for all that Helen says. It's just the first signs of good business sense.

I put the block over to one side of the desk and went on with the checks. The next day, during lunch hour, I bought some more stamps so I could mail them. And off and on, all day, I wondered what could have happened to that sheet of stamps.

I didn't think at all about the block that had the oily feel. Possibly I would have forgotten it entirely, except that when I got home, the fountain pen was missing.

I went into the den to get the pen and there the pen was, lying on top of the desk where I'd left it the night before. Not that I remembered leaving it there. But when I saw it there, I remembered having forgotten to put it back into the drawer.

I picked it up. It wasn't any pen. It felt like a cylinder of cork, but much too heavy to be any kind of cork. Except that it was heavier and smaller, it felt something—somehow—like a fly rod.

Thinking of how a fly rod felt, I gave my hand a twitch, the way you do to cast a line, and suddenly it seemed to be, in fact, a fly rod. It apparently had been telescoped and now it came untelescoped and lengthened out into what might have been a rod. But the funny thing about it was that it went out only about four feet and then disappeared into thin air.

Instinctively, I brought it up and back to free the tip from wherever it might be. I felt the slack take up against a sudden weight and I knew I had something on the other end of it. Just like a fish feels, only it wasn't fighting.

Then, as quickly as it happened, it unhappened. I felt the tension snap off and the weight at the other end was gone and the rod had telescoped again and I held in my hand the thing that looked like a fountain pen.

I laid it down carefully on the desk, being very certain to make no more casting motions, and it wasn't until then that I saw my hand was shaking.

I sat down, goggling at the thing that looked like the missing fountain pen and the other thing that looked like a Bildo-Block.

And it was then, while I was looking at the two of them, that I saw, out of the corner of my eye, the little white dot in the center of the desk.

It was on the exact spot where the bogus pen had lain and more than likely, I imagined, the exact spot where I'd found the Bildo-Block the night before. It was about a quarter of an inch in diameter and it looked like ivory.

I put out my thumb and rubbed it vigorously, but the dot would not rub off. I closed my eyes so the dot would have a chance to go away, and then opened them again, real quick, to surprise it if it hadn't. It still was there.

I bent over the desk to examine it. I could see it was inlaid in the wood, and an excellent job of inlaying, too. I couldn't find even the faintest line of division between the wood and the dot.

10

It hadn't been there before; I was sure of that. If it had been, I would have noticed it. What's more, Helen would have noticed it, for she's hell on dirt and forever after things with a dusting cloth. And to cinch the fact that it had not been there before, no one I ever heard of sold desks with single inlaid ivory dots.

And no one sold a thing that looked like a fountain pen but could become a fly rod, the business end of which disappeared and hooked a thing you couldn't even see—and which, the next time, might bring in whatever it had caught instead of losing it.

Helen called to me from the living room. "Joe."

"Yeah. What is it?"

"Did you talk to Bill?"

"Bill? About what?"

"About the trading."

"No. I guess I forgot."

"Well, you'll have to. He's at it again. He traded Jimmy out of that new bicycle. Gave him a lot of junk. I made him give back the bicycle."

"I'll have a talk with him," I promised again.

But I'm afraid I wasn't paying as close attention to the ethics of the situation as I should have been.

You couldn't keep a thing around the house. You were always losing this or that. You knew just where you'd put it and you were sure it was there and then, when you went to look for it, it had disappeared.

It was happening everywhere—things being lost and never turning up.

But other things weren't left in their places—at least not that you heard about.

Although maybe there had been times when things had been left that a man might pick up and examine and not know what they were and puzzle over, then toss in a corner somewhere and forget.

Maybe, I thought, the junkyards of the world were loaded with outlandish blocks and crazy fishing rods.

I got up and went into the living room, where Helen had turned on the television set.

She must have seen that something had me upset, because she asked, "What's the matter now?"

"I can't find the fountain pen."

She laughed at me. "Honestly, Joe, you're the limit. You're always losing things."

That night, I lay awake after Helen went to sleep and all I could think about was the dot upon the desk. A dot, perhaps, that said: *Put it right here, pardner, and we will make a swap.*

And, thinking of it, I wondered what would happen if someone moved the desk.

I lay there for a long time, trying not to worry, trying to tell myself it didn't matter, that I was insane to think what I was thinking.

But I couldn't get it out of my mind.

So I finally got up and sneaked out of the bedroom and, feeling like a thief in my own house, headed for the den.

I closed the door, turned on the desk lamp and took a quick look to see if the dot was still there.

It was.

I opened the desk drawer and hunted for a pencil and couldn't find one, but I finally found one of Bill's crayons. I got down on my knees and carefully marked the floor around the desk legs, so that, if the desk were moved, I could put it back again.

Then, pretending I had no particular purpose for doing it, I laid the crayon precisely on the dot.

In the morning, I sneaked a look into the den and the crayon was still there. I went to work a little easier in my mind, for by then I'd managed to convince myself that it was all imagination.

But that evening, after dinner, I went back into the den and the crayon was gone.

In its place was a triangular contraption with what appeared to be lenses set in each angle, and with a frame-

12

work of some sort of metal, holding in place what apparently was a suction cup in the center of the triangle.

While I was looking at it, Helen came to the door. "Marge and I are going to see a movie," she said. "Why don't you go over and have a beer with Lewis?"

"With that stuffed shirt?"

"What's the matter with Lewis?"

"Nothing, I guess." I didn't feel up to a family row right then.

"What's that you've got?" she asked.

"I don't know. Just something I found."

"Well, don't *you* start bringing home all sorts of junk, the way Bill does. One of you is enough to clutter up the house."

I sat there, looking at the triangle, and the only thing I could figure out was that it might be a pair of glasses. The suction cup in the center might hold it on the wearer's face and, while that might seem a funny way to wear a pair of glasses, it made sense when you thought about it. But if that were true, it meant that the wearer had three eyes, set in a triangle in his face.

I sat around for quite a while after Helen left, doing a lot of thinking. And what I was thinking was that even if I didn't care too much about Lewis, he was the only man I knew who might be able to help me out.

So I put the bogus fountain pen and the three-eyed glasses in the drawer and put the counterfeit Bildo-Block in my pocket and went across the street.

Lewis had a bunch of blueprints spread out on the kitchen table, and he started to explain them to me. I did the best I could to act as if I understood them. Actually, I didn't know head nor tail of it.

Finally, I was able to get a word in edgewise and I pulled the block out of my pocket and put it on the table.

"What is that?" I asked.

I expected him to say right off it was just a child's block. But he didn't. There must have been something about it

13

to tip him off that it wasn't just a simple block. That comes, of course, of having a technical education.

Lewis picked the block up and turned it around in his fingers. "What's it made of?" he asked me, sounding excited.

I shook my head. "I don't know what it is or what it's made of or anything about it. I just found it."

"This is something I've never seen before." Then he spotted the depression in one side of it and I could see I had him hooked. "Let me take it down to the shop. We'll see what we can learn."

I knew what he was after, of course. If the block was something new, he wanted a chance to go over it—but that didn't bother me any. I had a hunch he wouldn't find out too much about it.

We had a couple more beers and I went home. I hunted up an old pair of spectacles and put them on the desk right over the dot.

I was listening to the news when Helen came in. She said she was glad I'd spent the evening with Lewis, that I should try to get to know him better and that, once I got to know him better, I might like him. She said, since she and Marge were such good friends, it was a shame Lewis and I didn't hit it off.

"Maybe we will," I said and let it go at that.

The next afternoon, Lewis called me at the office.

"Where'd you get that thing?" he asked.

"Found it," I said.

"Have any idea what it is?"

"Nope," I told him cheerfully. "That's why I gave it to you."

"It's powered in some way and it's meant to measure something. That depression in the side must be a gauge. Color seems to be used as an indicator. At any rate, the color line in the depression keeps changing all the time. Not much, but enough so you can say there's some change."

"Next thing is to find out what it's measuring."

"Joe, do you know where you can get another of them?"

"No, I don't."

"It's this way," he said. "We'd like to get into this one, to see what makes it tick, but we can't find any way to open it. We could break into it, probably, but we're afraid to do that. We might damage it. Or it might explode. If we had another . . ."

"Sorry, Lewis. I don't know where to get another."

He had to let it go at that.

I went home that evening grinning to myself, thinking about Lewis. The guy was fit to be tied. He wouldn't sleep until he found out what the thing was, now that he'd started on it. It probably would keep him out of my hair for a week or so.

I went into the den. The glasses still were on the desk. I stood there for a moment, looking at them, wondering what was wrong. Then I saw that the lenses had a pinkish shade.

I picked them up, noticing that the lenses had been replaced by the kind in the triangular pair I had found there the night before.

Just then, Helen came into the room and I could tell, even before she spoke, that she had been waiting for me.

"Joe Adams," she demanded, "what have you been up to?"

"Not a thing," I told her.

"Marge says you got Lewis all upset."

"It doesn't take a lot to upset him."

"There's something going on," she insisted, "and I want to know what it is."

I knew I was licked. "I've been trading."

"Trading! After all I've said about Bill!"

"But this is different."

"Trading is trading," she said flatly.

Bill came in the front door, but he must have heard his mother say "trading," for he ducked out again. I yelled for him to come back.

"I want both of you to sit down and listen to me," I

said. "You can ask questions and offer suggestions and give me hell after I'm through."

So we sat down, all three of us, and had a family pow-wow.

It took quite a bit to make Helen believe what I had to tell, but I pointed out the dot in the desk and showed them the triangular glasses and the pair of glasses that had been refitted with the pink lenses and sent back to me. By that time, she was ready to admit there was something going on. Even so, she was fairly well burned up at me for marking up the floor around the desk legs.

I didn't show either her or Bill the pen that was a fishing rod, for I was scared of that. Flourish it around a bit and there was no telling what would happen.

Bill was interested and excited, of course. This was trading, which was right down his alley.

I cautioned both of them not to say a word about it. Bill wouldn't, for he was hell on secrets and special codes. But bright and early in the morning, Helen would probably swear Marge to secrecy, then tell her all about it and there wasn't a thing that I could do or say to stop her.

Bill wanted to put the pink-lensed spectacles on right away, to see how they were different from any other kind. I wouldn't let him. I wanted to put those specs on myself, but I was afraid to, if you want to know the truth.

When Helen went out to the kitchen to get dinner, Bill and I held a strategy session. For a ten-year-old, Bill had a lot of good ideas. We agreed that we ought to get some system into the trading, because, as Bill pointed out, the idea of swapping sight unseen was a risky sort of business. A fellow ought to have some say in what he was getting in return.

But to arrive at an understanding with whoever we were trading with meant that we'd have to set up some sort of communication system. And how do you communicate with someone you don't know the first thing about, except that perhaps it has three eyes?

Then Bill hit upon what seemed a right idea. What we

16

needed, he said, was a catalogue. If you were going to trade with someone, the logical first step would be to let them know what you had to trade.

To be worth anything in such a circumstance, it would have to be an illustrated catalogue. And even then it might be worthless, for how could we be sure that the Trader on the other side of the desk would know what a picture was? Maybe he'd never seen a picture before. Maybe he saw differently—not so much physically, although that was possible, too, but from a different viewpoint and with totally alien concepts.

But it was the only thing we had to go on, so we settled down to work up a catalogue. Bill thought we should draw one, but neither of us was any good at drawing. I suggested illustrations from magazines. But that wasn't too hot an idea, either, for pictures of items in the magazine ads are usually all prettied up, designed to catch the eye.

Then Bill had a top-notch idea. "You know that kid dictionary Aunt Ethel gave me? Why don't we send that to them? It's got a lot of pictures and not much reading in it, and that's important. The reading might confuse them."

So we went into his room and started looking through all the junk he had, searching for the dictionary. But we ran across one of the old ABC books he'd had when he was just a toddler and decided it was even better than the dictionary. It had good clear pictures and almost no reading at all. You know the kind of book I mean—A for apple, B for ball and so forth.

We took the book into the den and put it on the desk, centering it on the dot, then went out to dinner.

In the morning the book had disappeared and that was a little odd. Up until then, nothing had disappeared from the desk until late in the day.

Early that afternoon, Lewis called me up. "I'm coming down to see you, Joe. Is there a bar handy where the two of us can be alone?"

I told him there was one only a block from me and said I'd meet him there.

I got a few things cleared away, then left the office, figuring I'd go over to the bar and have a quick one before Lewis showed up.

I don't know how he did it, but he was there ahead of me, back in a corner booth. He must have broken every traffic regulation on the books.

He had a couple of drinks waiting for us and was all huddled over, like a conspirator. He was a bit out of breath, as he had every right to be.

"Marge told me," he said.

"I suspected she would."

"There could be a mint in it, Joe!"

"That's what I thought, too. That's why I'm willing to give you ten per cent . . ."

"Now look here," squawked Lewis. "You can't pull a deal like that. I wouldn't touch it for less than fifty."

"I'm letting you in on it," I said, "because you're a neighbor. I don't know beans about this technical business. I'm getting stuff I don't understand and I need some help to find out what it is, but I can always go to someone else . . ."

It took us three drinks to get the details settled—35 per cent for him, 65 for me.

"Now that that's settled," I said, "suppose you tell me what you found."

"Found?"

"That block I gave you. You wouldn't have torn down here and had the drinks all set up and waiting if you hadn't found something."

"Well, as a matter of fact . . ."

"Now just a minute," I warned him. "We're going to put this in the contract—any failure to provide full and complete analysis . . ."

"What contract?"

"We're going to have a contract drawn up, so either of

us can sue the other within an inch of his life for breaking it."

Which is a hell of a way to start out a business venture, but it's the only way to handle a slippery little skate like Lewis.

So he told me what he'd found. "It's an emotions gauge. That's awkward terminology, I know, but it's the best I can think of."

"What does it do?"

"It tells how happy you are or how sad or how much you hate someone."

"Oh, great," I said, disappointed. "What good is a thing like that? I don't need a gauge to tell me if I'm sore or glad or anything."

He waxed practically eloquent. "Don't you see what an instrument like that would mean to psychiatrists? It would tell more about patients than they'd ever be willing to tell about themselves. It could be used in mental institutions and it might be important in gauging reactions for the entertainment business, politics, law-enforcement and Lord knows what else."

"No kidding! Then let's start marketing!"

"The only thing is . . ."

"Yes?"

"We can't manufacture them," he said frustratedly. "We haven't got the materials and we don't know how they're made. You'll have to trade for them."

"I can't. Not right away, that is. First I've got to be able to make the Traders understand what I want, and then I'll have to find out what they're willing to trade them for."

"You have some other stuff?"

"A few things."

"You better turn them over to me."

"Some that could be dangerous. Anyhow, it all belongs to me. I'll give you what I want, when I want and . . ."

We were off again.

We finally wound up by adjourning to an attorney's office.

19

We wrote up a contract that is probably one of the legal curiosities of all time.

I'm convinced the attorney thought, and still thinks, both of us are crazy, but that's the least of my worries now.

The contract said I was to turn over to Lewis, for his determination of its technical and merchandisable nature, at least 90 per cent of certain items, the source of which I alone controlled, and with the further understanding that said source was to remain at all times under my exclusive control. The other 10 per cent might, without prejudice, be withheld from his examination, with the party of the first part having sole authority to make determination of which items should constitute the withheld 10 per cent.

Upon the 90 per cent of the items supplied him, the party of the second part was to make a detailed analysis, in writing, accompanied by such explanatory material as was necessary to the complete understanding of the party of the first part, within no more than three months after receipt, at the end of which time the items reverted solely to the ownership of the party of the first part. Except that such a period of examination and determination might be extended, under a mutual agreement made in writing, for any stated time.

Under no circumstances should the party of the second part conceal from the party of the first part any findings he might have made upon any of the items covered by the agreement, and that such concealment, should it occur, should be considered sufficient cause for action for the recovery of damages. That under certain conditions where some of the items might be found to be manufacturable, they could be manufactured under the terms of clauses A, B and C, section XII of this agreement.

Provisions for a sales organization to market any of said items shall be set up and made a part of this agreement. That any proceeds from such sales shall be divided as follows: 65 per cent to the party of the first part (me, in case you've gotten lost, which is understandable), and 35 per cent to the party of the second part (Lewis); costs to be apportioned accordingly.

There were a lot more details, of course, but that gives you an idea.

We got home from the attorney's office, without either of us knifing the other, and found Marge over at my place. Lewis went in with me to have a look at the desk.

Apparently the Trader had received the ABC book all right and had been able to understand why it was sent, for there, lying on the desk, was a picture cut out of the book. Well, not cut out, exactly—it looked more as though it had been burned out.

The picture on the desk was Z for zebra.

Lewis stared worriedly at it. "Now we're really in a fix."

"Yeah," I admitted. "I don't know what the market price is, but they can't be cheap."

"Figure it out—expedition, safari, cages, ship, rail, fodder, keeper. You think we can switch him to something else?"

"I don't see how. He's put in his order."

Bill came wandering in and wanted to know what was up. When I glumly told him, he said cheerfully, "Aw, that's the whole trick in trading, Pop. If you got a bum jackknife you want to trade, you unload it on somebody who doesn't know what a good knife is like."

Lewis didn't get it, but I did. "That's right! He doesn't know a zebra is an animal, or, if he does, how big it is!"

"Sure," Bill said confidently. "All he saw was a picture."

It was five o'clock then, but the three of us went uptown and shopped. Bill found a cheap bracelet charm about the size of the drawing in the book. When it comes to junk like that, my kid knows just where it's sold and how much it costs. I considered making him a junior partner in charge of such emergencies, with about 10 per cent share or so— out of Lewis's 35 per cent, of course—but I was sure Lewis wouldn't hold still for that. I decided instead to give Bill a dollar a week allowance, said compensation to commence immediately upon our showing a profit.

Well, we had Z for zebra—provided the Trader was

satisfied with a little piece of costume jewelry. It was lucky, I thought, that it hadn't been Z for zephyr.

The rest of the alphabet was easy, yet I couldn't help but kick myself over all the time we were wasting. Of all the unworthy catalogues we might have sent, that ABC book was the worst. But until the Trader had run through the whole list, I was afraid to send another for fear of confusing him.

So I sent him an apple and a ball and a small doll for a girl and toy cat and toy dog, and so on, and then I lay awake nights wondering what the Trader would make of them. I could picture him trying to learn the use of a rubber doll or cat.

I'd given Lewis the two pairs of glasses, but had held back the fountain-pen fishing rod, for I was still scared of that one. He had turned over the emotion gauge to a psychiatrist to try out in his practice as a sort of field test.

Marge and Helen, knowing that Lewis and I had entered into some kind of partnership, were practically inseparable now. Helen kept telling me how glad she was that I had finally recognized what a sterling fellow Lewis was. I suppose Lewis heard the same thing about me from Marge.

Bill went around practically busting to do some bragging. But Bill is a great little businessman and he kept his mouth shut. I told him about the allowance, of course.

Lewis was all for trying to ask the Trader for a few more of the emotion gauges. He had a draftsman at the plant draw up a picture of the gauge and he wanted me to send it through to indicate that we were interested in it.

But I told him not to try to rush things. While the emotion gauge might be a good deal, we should sample what the Trader had to offer before we made up our minds.

The Trader, apparently certain now that someone was co-operating with him, had dropped his once-a-day trade schedule and was open for business around the clock. After he had run through the list in the ABC book, he sent back a couple of blank pages from the book with very crude drawings on them—drawings that looked as if they had been made with crumbly charcoal. Lewis drew a series of pictures, showing how a pencil worked, and we sent the Trader a ream of paper and a gross of sharpened pencils, then sat back to wait.

We waited a week and were getting sort of edgy, when back came the entire ream of paper, with each sheet covered on both sides with all kinds of drawings. So we sent him a mail-order catalogue, figuring that would hold him for a while, and settled down to try to puzzle out the drawings he had made.

There wasn't a single thing that made any sense at all— not even to Lewis. He'd study some of the drawings, then pace up and down the room, pulling his hair and twitching his ears. Then he'd study the drawings some more.

To me, it all looked plain Rube Goldbergish.

Finally, we figured we might as well forget about the catalogue idea, for the time being at least, and we started feeding all sorts of stuff through the desk—scissors, dishes, shoes, jackknives, mucilage, cigars, paper clips, erasers, spoons—almost anything that was handy. It wasn't the scientific way, I know, but we didn't have the time to get very methodical about it and, until we had a chance to work out a more sensible program, we figured we might as well try the shotgun method.

And the Trader started shooting things back at us. We'd sit for hours and feed stuff through to him and then he'd shoot stuff back at us and we had the damnedest pile of junk heaped all over the place you ever laid eyes on.

We rigged up a movie camera and took a lot of film of the spot on the desk where the exchange was going on. We spent a lot of time viewing that film, slowing it down and even stopping it, but it didn't tell us anything at all. When the stuff disappeared or appeared, it just disappeared or appeared. One frame it would be there, the next frame it would be gone.

Lewis canceled all his other work and used the lab for nothing but trying to puzzle out the gadgets that we got.

23

Most of them we couldn't crack at all. I imagine they were useful in some way, but we never managed to learn how.

There was the perfume bottle, for example. That is what we called it, anyhow. But there was a suspicion in our minds that the perfume was simply a secondary effect, that the so-called bottle was designed for some other purpose entirely.

Lewis and his boys were studying it down at the lab, trying to make out some rhyme or reason for it, and somehow they turned it on. They worked for three days, the last two in gas masks, trying to turn it off again. When the smell got so bad that people began calling the police, we took the contraption out into the country and buried it. Within a few days, all the vegetation in the area was dead. All the rest of the summer, the boys from the agricultural department at the university ran around, practically frothing at the mouth, trying to find the cause.

There was the thing that might have been a clock of some sort, although it might just as easily have been something else. If it was a clock, the Trader had a time system that would drive you nuts, for it would measure the minutes or hours or whatever they were like lightning for a while, then barely move for an entire day.

And there was the one you'd point at something and press a certain spot on it—not a button or a knob or anything as crass and mechanical as that, just a certain spot— and there'd be just a big blank spot in the landscape. But when you stopped pressing, the landscape would come back again, unchanged. We filed it away in the darkest corner of the laboratory safe, with a big red tag on it marked: *Dangerous! Don't Monkey with This!*

But most of the items we just drew blanks on. And it kept coming all the time. I piled the garage full of it and started dumping it in the basement. Some of it I was scared of and hauled out to the dump.

In the meantime, Lewis was having trouble with the emotion gauge. "It works," he said. "The psychiatrist I

24

gave it to to try out is enthusiastic about it. But it seems almost impossible to get it on the market."

"If it works," I objected, handing him a can of beer, "it ought to sell."

"In any other field, it might, but you don't handle merchandise that way in the medical field. Before you can put something on the market, you have to have it nailed down with blueprints and theory and field tests and such. And we can't. We don't know *how* it works. We don't know *why* it works. Until we do, no reputable medical supply house will take it on, no approved medical journal will advertise it, no practitioner will use it."

"Then I guess it's out." I felt fairly blue about it, because it was the only thing we had that we knew how to use.

Lewis nodded and drank his beer and was glummer than ever.

Looking back on it, it's funny how we found the gadget that made us all the money. Actually, it wasn't Lewis but Helen who found it.

Helen is a good housewife. She's always going after things with the vacuum and the dustcloth and she washes the woodwork so often and so furiously that we have to paint it every year.

One night, we were sitting in the living room, watching television.

"Joe," she asked me, "did you dust the den?"

"Dust the den? What would I want to do that for?"

"Well, someone did. Maybe it was Bill."

"Bill wouldn't be caught dead with a dustcloth in his mitt."

"I can't understand it, Joe," she said. "I went in there to dust it and it was absolutely clean. Everything just shone."

Sgt. Friday was trying to get the facts out of someone and his sidekick was complaining about some relatives that had come to visit and I didn't pay much attention at the time.

25

But the next day, I got to thinking about it and I couldn't get it off my mind. I certainly hadn't dusted the den and it was a cinch Bill hadn't, yet someone had if Helen was ready to admit it was clean.

So, that evening, I went out into the street with a pail and shoveled up a pailful of dirt and brought it in the house.

Helen caught me as I was coming in the door. "What do you think you're doing with that?"

"Experimenting," I told her.

"Do it in the garage."

"It isn't possible," I argued. "I have to find out who's been dusting the den."

I knew that, if my hunch failed, I'd have a lot to answer for when she followed me and stood in the doorway, ready to pounce.

There was a bunch of junk from the Trader standing on the desk and a lot more of it in one corner. I cleared off the desk and that was when Bill came in.

"What you doing, Dad?" he asked.

"Your father's gone insane," Helen explained quietly.

They stood there, watching me, while I took a handful of dirt and sprinkled on the desk top.

It stayed there for just an instant—and then it was gone. The top of the desk was spotless.

"Bill," I said, "take one of those gadgets out to the garage."

"Which one?"

"It doesn't matter."

So he took one and I spread another handful of dirt and, in a second, it was gone.

Bill was back by that time and I sent him out with another gadget.

We kept on like that for quite a while and Bill was beginning to get disgusted with me. But finally I sprinkled the dirt and it stayed.

"Bill," I said, "you remember the last thing you took out?"

"Sure."

"Well, go out and bring it back again."

He got it and, as soon as he reached the door of the den, the dirt disappeared.

"Well, that's it," I said.

"That's what?" asked Helen.

I pointed to the contraption Bill had in his hand. "That. Throw away your vacuum cleaner. Burn up the dustcloth. Heave out the mop. Just have one of those in the house and . . ."

She threw herself into my arms.

"Oh, *Joe!*"

We danced a jig, the two of us.

Then I sat around for a while, kicking myself for tying up with Lewis, wondering if maybe there wasn't some way I could break the contract now that I had found something without any help from him. But I remembered all those clauses we had written in. It wouldn't have been any use, anyhow, for Helen was already across the street, telling Marge about it.

So I phoned Lewis at the lab and he came tearing over. We ran field tests.

The living room was spotless from Bill just having walked through it, carrying the gadget, and the garage, where he had taken it momentarily, was spic and span. While we didn't check it, I imagine that an area paralleling the path he had taken from the front door to the garage was the only place outdoors that didn't have a speck of dust upon it.

We took the gadget down in the basement and cleaned that up. We sneaked over to a neighbor's back yard, where we knew there was a lot of cement dust, held the gadget over it and in an instant there wasn't any cement dust. There were just a few pebbles left and the pebbles, I suppose, you couldn't rightly classify as dust.

We didn't need to know any more.

Back at the house, I broke open a bottle of Scotch I'd been saving, while Lewis sat down at the kitchen table and drew a sketch of the gadget.

We had a drink, then went into the den and put the drawing on the desk. The drawing disappeared and we waited. In a few minutes, another one of the gadgets appeared. We waited for a while and nothing happened.

"We've got to let him know we want a lot of them," I said.

"There's no way we can," said Lewis. "We don't know his mathematical symbols, he doesn't know ours, and there's no sure-fire way to teach him. He doesn't know a single word of our language and we don't know a word of his."

We went back to the kitchen and had another drink.

Lewis sat down and drew a row of the gadgets across a sheet of paper, then sketched in representations of others behind them so that, when you looked at it, you could see that there were hundreds of them.

We sent that through.

Fourteen gadgets came back—the exact number Lewis had sketched in the first row.

Apparently the Trader had no idea of perspective. The lines that Lewis had drawn to represent the other gadgets behind the first row didn't mean a thing to him.

We went back to the kitchen and had a few more drinks.

"We'll need thousands of the things," said Lewis, holding his head in his hands. "I can't sit here day and night, drawing them."

"You may have to do that," I said, enjoying myself.

"There *must* be another way."

"Why not draw a bunch of them, then mimeograph the drawing?" I suggested. "We could send the mimeograph sheets through to him in bundles."

I hated to say it, because I was still enamored of the idea of sticking Lewis somewhere off in a corner, sentenced to a lifetime of drawing the same thing over and over.

"That might work," said Lewis, brightening annoyingly. "It's just simple enough . . ."

"Practical is the word," I snapped. "If it were simple, you'd have thought of it."

"I leave things like that to detail men."

"You'd better!"

It took a while and a whole bottle before we calmed down.

Next day, we bought a mimeograph machine and Lewis drew a stencil with twenty-five of the gadgets on it. We ran through a hundred sheets and sent them through the desk.

It worked—we were busy for several hours, getting those gadgets out of the way as they poured through to us.

I'm afraid we never stopped to think about what the Trader might want in return for the dust-collectors. We were so excited that we forgot, for the moment, that this was a commercial proposition and not just something gratis.

But the next afternoon, back came the mimeographed sheets we'd sent through and, on the reverse side of each of them, the Trader had drawn twenty-five representations of the zebra bracelet charm.

And there we were, faced with the necessity of getting together pronto, twenty-five hundred of those silly zebras.

I tore down to the store where I'd gotten the bracelet, but all they had in stock were two dozen of the things. They said they didn't think they could order any more. The number, they said, had been discontinued.

The name of the company that made them was stamped on the inside of the bracelet and, as soon as I got home, I put in a long distance call.

I finally got hold of the production manager. "You know those bracelets you put out?"

"We put out millions of 'em. Which one are you talking about?"

"The one with the zebra on it."

He thought a moment. "Yeah, we did. Quite a while ago. We don't make them any more. In this business . . ."

"I need at least twenty-five hundred of them."

"Twenty-five hundred bracelets?"

"No, just the zebras."

"Look, is this a gag?"

"It's no gag, mister," I said. "I need those zebras. I'm willing to pay for them."

"We haven't any in stock."

"Couldn't you make them?"

"Not just twenty-five hundred of them. Wouldn't be worth it to put through a special order for so few. If it was fifty thousand, say, we might consider it."

"All right, then," I said. "How much for fifty thousand?"

He named a price and we haggled some, but I was in no position to do much bargaining. We finally agreed on a price I knew was way too high, considering the fact that the entire bracelet, with the zebra and a lot of other junk, had only retailed at 39 cents.

"And hold the order open," I told him. "We might want more of them."

"Okay," he said. "Just one thing—would you mind telling me what you want with fifty thousand zebras?"

"Yes, I would," I said and hung up.

I suppose he thought I was off my rocker, but who cared what he thought?

It took ten days to get that shipment of fifty thousand zebras and I sweated out every minute of it. Then there was the job of getting them under cover when it came and, in case you don't know, fifty thousand zebras, even when they're only bracelet charms, take up room.

But first I took out twenty-five hundred and sent them through the desk.

For the ten days since we'd gotten the dust-collectors, we'd sent nothing through and there had been no sign from the Trader that he might be getting impatient. I wouldn't have blamed him a bit if he'd done something, like sending through his equivalent of a bomb, to express his dissatisfaction at our slow delivery. I've often wondered what he thought of the long delay—if he hadn't suspected we were reneging on the bargain.

All this time, I had been smoking too much and gnawing my fingernails and I'd figured that Lewis was just as busy seeing what could be done about marketing the dusters.

30

But when I mentioned it to him he just looked blank. "You know, Joe, I've been doing a lot of worrying."

"We haven't a thing to worry about now," I said, "except getting these things sold."

"But the dust must go somewhere," he fretted.

"The dust?"

"Sure, the dust these things collect. Remember we picked up an entire pile of cement dust? What I want to know is where it all went. The gadget itself isn't big enough to hold it. It isn't big enough to hold even a week's collection of dust from the average house. That's what worries me—where does it go?"

"I don't care where. It goes, doesn't it?"

"That's the pragmatic view," he said scornfully.

It turned out that Lewis hadn't done a thing about marketing, so I got busy.

But I ran into the same trouble we'd had trying to sell the emotion gauge.

The dust collector wasn't patented and it didn't have a brand name. There was no fancy label stuck on it and it didn't bear a manufacturer's imprint. And when anybody asked me how it worked, I couldn't answer.

One wholesaler did make me a ridiculous offer. I laughed in his face and walked out.

That night, Lewis and I sat around the kitchen table, drinking beer, and neither of us too happy. I could see a lot of trouble ahead in getting the gadgets sold. Lewis, it seemed, was still worrying about what happened to the dust.

He had taken one of the dust collectors apart and the only thing he could find out about it was that there was some feeble force-field operating inside of it—feeble yet strong enough to play hell with the electrical circuits and fancy metering machinery he has at the lab. As soon as he found out what was happening, he slapped the cover back on as quick as he could and then everything was all right. The cover was a shield against the force-field.

31

"That dust must be getting thrown into another dimension," he told me, looking like a hound dog that had lost a coon track.

"Maybe not. It could be winding up in one of those dust clouds way out in space."

He shook his head.

"You can't tell me," I said, "that the Trader is crazy enough to sell us a gadget that will throw dust back into his face."

"You miss the point entirely. The Trader is operating from another dimension. He *must* be. And if there are two dimensions, his and ours, there may be others. The Trader must have used these dust collectors himself—not for the same purpose we intend, perhaps, but they get rid of something that he doesn't want around. So, necessarily, they'd have to be rigged to get rid of it in a dimension other than his."

We sat there drinking beer and I started turning over that business about different dimensions in my head. I couldn't grasp the concept. Maybe Lewis was right about me being a pragmatist. If you can't see it or touch it or even guess what it would be like, how can you believe there might be another dimension? I couldn't.

So I started to talk about marketing the dust collector and before Lewis went home that night, we'd decided that the only thing left to do was sell it door to door. We even agreed to charge $12.50 for it. The zebras figured out to four cents each and we would pay our salesmen ten per cent commission, which would leave us a profit of $11.21 apiece.

I put an ad in the paper for salesmen and the next day we had several applicants. We started them out on a trial run.

Those gadgets sold like hotcakes and we knew we were in!

I quit my job and settled down to handling the sales end, while Lewis went back to the lab and started going through the pile of junk we had gotten from the Trader.

There are a lot of headaches running a sales campaign. You have to map out territories for your salesmen, get clearance from Better Business Bureaus, bail out your men if they're thrown in the clink for running afoul of some obscure village ordinance. There are more worrisome angles to it than you can ever imagine.

But in a couple of months' time, things were running pretty smoothly. We had the state well covered and were branching out into others. I had ordered another fifty thousand zebras and told them to expect re-orders—and the desk top was a busy place. It got to a point, finally, where I had to hire three men full time, paying them plenty not to talk, to man that desk top twenty-four hours a day. We'd send through zebras for eight hours, then take away dust gadgets for eight hours, then feed through zebras for another eight.

If the Trader had any qualms about what was happening, he gave no sign of it. He seemed perfectly happy to send us dust collectors so long as we sent him zebras.

The neighbors were curious and somewhat upset at first, but finally they got used to it. If I could have moved to some other location, I would have, for the house was more an office than a home and we had practically no family life at all. But if we wanted to stay in business, we had to stay right where we were because it was the only place we had contact with the Trader.

The money kept rolling in and I turned the management of it over to Helen and Marge. The income tax boys gave us a rough time when we didn't show any manufacturing expenses, but since we weren't inclined to argue over what we had to pay, they couldn't do anything about it.

Lewis was wearing himself down to a nubbin at the lab, but he wasn't finding anything that we could use.

But he still did some worrying now and then about where all that dust was going. And he was right, probably for the first time in his life.

One afternoon, a couple of years after we'd started selling

the dust collectors, I had been uptown to attend to some banking difficulties that Helen and Marge had gotten all bollixed up. I'd no more than pulled into the driveway when Helen came busting out of the house. She was covered with dust, her face streaked with it, and she was the maddest-looking woman I have ever seen.

"You've got to do something about it Joe!" she shrieked.

"About what?"

"The dust! It's pouring into the house!"

"Where is it pouring from?"

"From *everywhere!*"

I could see she'd opened all the windows and there was dust pouring out of them, almost like a smoke cloud. I got out of the car and took a quick look up and down the street. Every house in the block had its windows open and there was dust coming out of all of them and the neighborhood was boiling with angry, screaming women.

"Where's Bill?" I asked

"Out back."

I ran around the house and called him and he came running.

Marge had come across the street and, if anything, she was about six degrees sorer about all the dust than Helen was.

"Get in the car," I said.

"Where are we going?" Marge demanded.

"Out to pick up Lewis."

I must have sounded like nothing to trifle with, for they piled in and I got out of there as fast as the car would take us.

The homes and factories and stores that had bought the gadget were gushing so much dust, visibility wouldn't be worth a damn before long.

I had to wade through about two feet of dust on the laboratory floor to get to Lewis's office and hold a handkerchief over my nose to keep from suffocating.

Inside the car we got our faces wiped off and most of the

dust hacked out of our throats. I could see then that Lewis was about three shades paler than usual, although to tell the truth, he always was a pasty-looking creature.

"It's the creatures from the third dimension," he said anxiously. "The place where we were sending all the dust. They got sick and tired of having it pour in on them and they got it figured out and now they're firing the dust right back at us."

"Now calm down. We're just jumping at the conclusion that this was caused by our gadget."

"I checked, Joe. It was. The dust is coming out in jets from every single place where we sent it through. No place else."

"Then all we have to do it fire it back at them."

He shook his head. "Not a chance. The gadget works one way now—from them to us." He coughed and looked wildly at me. "Think of it! A couple of million homes, stores and factories—some of them operating for two whole years! Joe, what are we going to do?"

"We're going to hole up somewhere till this—well, blows over."

Being of a nasty legal turn of mind, he probably foresaw even then the countless lawsuits that would avalanche on us. Personally, I was more scared of being mobbed by angry women.

But that's all past history. We hid out till people had quieted down and then began trying to settle the suits out of court. We had a lot of money and were able to pay off most of them. The judgments against us still outstanding don't amount to more than a few hundred thousand. We could wipe that out pretty quickly if we'd just hit on something else as profitable as the cleaning gadget.

Lewis is working hard at it, but he isn't having any luck. And the Trader is gone now. As soon as we dared come home, I went into the house and had a look at the desk. The inlaid dot was gone. I tried putting something where it had been, but nothing happened.

35

What scared the Trader off? I'd give a lot to know. Meanwhile, there are some commercial prospects.

The rose-tinted glasses, for instance, that we call the Happiness Lenses. Put them on and you're happy as a clam. Almost every person on the face of the Earth would like a pair of them, so they could forget their troubles for a while. They would probably play hob with the liquor business.

The trouble is that we don't know how to make them and, now that the Trader's gone, we can't swap for them.

But there's one thing that keeps worrying me. I know I shouldn't let it bother me, but I can't keep it out of mind.

Just what did the Trader do with those couple of million zebras we sent him?

Carbon Copy

THE MAN WHO CAME into Homer Jackson's office was wearing his left shoe on his right foot and his right shoe on his left.

He gave Homer quite a start.

The man was tall and had a gangling look about him, but he was smartly dressed—except for his shoes. And his shoes were all right, too; it was just the way he wore them.

"Am I addressing Mr. Homer Jackson?" he asked with a formality to which Homer was entirely unaccustomed.

"That's me," said Homer.

He squirmed a bit uncomfortably in his chair. He hoped this wasn't one of Gabby Wilson's jokes.

Gabby had an office just down the hall and loved to pester Homer plenty. When Gabby cooked up a joke, he did a massive job on it; he left out not a single detail. And some of Gabby's jokes got pretty rough.

But the man seemed to be dead serious and perhaps a little anxious.

"Mr. Homer Jackson, the suburban realtor?" he persisted.

"That's right," said Homer.

"Specializing in lake properties and country acreages?"

"I'm your man." Homer began to feel uncomfortable. This man was spreading it on a trifle thick and Homer thought he could see Gabby's hand in it.

"I'd like to talk with you. I have a matter of small business."

"Fire away," said Homer, motioning toward a chair.

The man sat down carefully, bolt upright in the chair.

"My name is Oscar Steen," he said. "We're building a development on what is known as the Saunders place. We call it Happy Acres."

Homer nodded. "I'm acquainted with the place. It's the last good holding on the lake. You were fortunate to get it."

"Thank you, Mr. Jackson. We think that it is nice."

"How are you getting on?"

"We have just finished it. But now comes the most important part. We must get people onto the property."

"Well," said Homer, "things are a little tough right now. Money has tightened up and the interest rates are higher and Washington is no help and besides that—"

"We wondered if you'd be interested in handling it for us."

Homer choked a little, but recovered quickly. "Well, now, I don't know. Those houses may be hard to sell. You'd have to get a solid figure for them and the prices will run high. That stone wall you put around the place and those fancy gates and all, I would suspect you have high-class houses. You have gone and made it into an exclusive section. There'll be only a certain class of buyer who might be interested."

"Mr. Jackson," said Steen, "we have a new approach. You won't have to sell them. We're only leasing them."

"Renting them, you mean."

"No, sir, leasing them."

"Well, it all comes out to the same thing in the end. You'll have to get a lot for them."

"Five thousand."

"Five thousand is an awful lot of money. At least, out here it is. Five thousand a year comes to over four hundred a month and—"

"Not for a year," corrected Steen. "For ninety-nine."

"For what!"

"Ninety-nine. We're leasing at five thousand dollars for ninety-nine full years."

"But, man, you can't do that! Why, that's absolutely crazy! Taxes would eat up—"

38

"We're not so interested in making money on the houses as we are in creating business for our shopping center."

"You mean you have a shopping center in there, too?"

Steen allowed himself a smile. "Mr. Jackson, we obtain the property and then we build the wall to have some privacy so there can be no snoopers."

"Yes, I know," said Homer. "It's smart to do it that way. Good publicity. Whets the public's interest. Gives you a chance to have a big unveiling. But that twelve-foot wall—"

"Fourteen, Mr. Jackson."

"All right, then, fourteen. And it's built of solid stone. I know—I watched them put it up. And no one builds walls of solid stone any more. They just use stone facing. The way you built that wall set you back a hunk—"

"Mr. Jackson, please. We know what we are doing. In this shopping center, we sell everything from peanuts to Cadillacs. But we need customers. So we build houses for our customers. We desire to create a good stable population of rather well-to-do families."

Jumping to his feet in exasperation, Homer paced up and down the office.

"But, Mr. Steen, you can't possibly build up enough business at your shopping center by relying solely on the people in your development. For instance, how many houses have you?"

"Fifty."

"Fifty families are a mere drop in the bucket for a shopping center. Even if every one of those fifty families bought all their needs from you—and you can't be sure they will—but if they did, you'd still have little volume. And you won't pick up any outside trade—not behind that wall, you won't."

He stopped his pacing and went back to his chair.

"I don't know why I'm upset about it," he told Steen. "It's no skin off my nose. Yes, I'll handle the development, but I can't handle leasing at my usual five per cent."

"Oh, I forgot to tell you," said Steen. "You keep the entire five thousand."

Homer gasped like a fish hauled suddenly from water.

"On one condition," added Steen. "One has to be so careful. We have a bank, you see. Part of the shopping center service."

"A bank," Homer said feebly.

"Chartered under the state banking regulations."

"And what has a bank to do with me?"

"You'll take ten per cent," said Steen. "The rest will be credited to your account in the Happy Acres Bank. Every time you lease a unit, you get five hundred cash; forty-five hundred goes in your bank account."

"I don't quite see—"

"There are advantages."

"Yes, I know," Homer said. "It builds up your business. You're out to make that shopping center go."

"That might be one factor. Another is that we can't have you getting rich in front of all your friends and neighbors. There'd be too much talk about it and we don't want that kind of publicity. And there are tax advantages as well."

"Tax advantages?"

"Mr. Jackson, if you lease all fifty houses, you will have earned a quarter million dollars. Have you figured what the income tax might be on a quarter million dollars?"

"It would be quite a lot."

"It would be a crying shame," said Steen. "The bank could be a help."

"I don't quite see how."

"You leave that to us. Leave everything to us. You just lease the houses."

"Mr. Steen, I've been an honest man for years in an occupation where there's opportunity—"

"Honesty, Mr. Jackson. Of course we know you're honest. That's why we came to you. Have you got your car here?"

"It's parked outside."

"Fine. Mine is at the station getting serviced. Let's drive out and look the houses over."

40

The houses were all that anyone could wish. They were planned with practical imagination and built with loving care. There was, Homer admitted to himself, more honest workmanship in them than he had seen for many years in this era of mass-production building. They had that quiet sense of quality material, of prideful craftsmanship, of solidity, of dignity and tradition that was seldom found any more.

They were well located, all fifty of them, in the wooded hills that stretched back from the lake, and the contractor had not indulged in the ruthless slashing out of trees. Set in natural surroundings with decent amounts of space around them, they stood, each one of them, in comparative privacy.

In the spring, there would be wild flowers, and in the autumn, the woods would flame with color and there would be birds and squirrels and rabbits. And there was a stretch of white sand beach, the last left on the whole lake.

Homer began mentally to write the ad he'd put in the Sunday paper and found that he looked forward with some anticipation to setting down the words. This was one he could pull out all the stops on, use all the purple prose he wanted.

"I like it, Mr. Steen," he said. "I think they won't be too hard to move."

"That is good," Steen replied. "We are prepared to give you an exclusive contract for a period of ten years. Renewable, of course."

"But why ten years? I can get this tract handled in a year or two, if it goes at all."

"You are mistaken. The business, I can assure you, will be continuing."

They stood on the brick walk in front of one of the houses and looked toward the lake. There were two white sails on the water, far toward the other shore, and a rowboat bobbed in the middle distance, with the black smudge of a hunched fisherman squatted in the stern.

Homer shook his head in some bewilderment. "I don't understand."

"There'll be some subletting," Steen told him smoothly. "When fifty families are involved, there are always some who move."

"But that's another story. Subletting—"

Steen pulled a paper from his pocket and handed it to Homer. "Your contract. You'll want to look it over. Look it over closely. You're a cautious man and that's the kind we want."

Homer drove along the winding, wooded road back to the shopping center with Steen.

The center was a lovely place. It stretched along the entire south side of the property, backed by the fourteen-foot wall, and was a shining place of brand-new paint and gleaming glass and metal.

Homer stopped the car to look at it.

"You've got everything," he said.

"I think we have," said Steen proudly. "We've even got our own telephone exchange."

"Isn't that unusual?"

"Not at all. What we have set up here amounts to a model village, a model living space. We have our own water system and our sewage plant. Why not a telephone exchange?"

Homer let it pass. There was no sense arguing. It all was just this side of crazy, anyhow. No matter how fouled up it was, Steen seemed satisfied.

Maybe, Homer told himself, he knows what he is doing.

But Homer doubted it.

"One thing more," said Steen. "It is just a minor matter, but you should know about it. We have a car agency, you see. Many agencies, in fact. We can supply almost any make of car—"

"But how did you do—"

"We know our way around. Any make of car a person would want. And anyone who leases must buy a car from us."

"Mister," Homer said, "I've heard a lot of fast ones in the auto business, but this one beats them all. If you think I'll sell cars for you—"

"There's nothing wrong with it," said Steen. "We have some good connections. Any car one wants at a fair and honest price. And we are prepared to give good value on their trade-ins, too. It would never do to have old rattle-traps in a high-class development like this."

"And what else? I think you better tell me how many other tie-in deals you have."

"Not a single one. The automobile is all."

Homer put the car in gear and drove slowly toward the gate.

The uniformed gateman saw them coming and swung the gates wide open. He waved to them cheerily as they went past his kiosk.

"I wouldn't touch it with a ten-foot pole," Homer told his wife, Elaine, "if there weren't so much money in it. But things have been kind of slow with this higher interest rate and all and this deal would give me a chance—"

"If it's Mr. Steen wearing his shoes on the wrong feet," Elaine said. "I don't think you need to worry. You remember Uncle Eb?"

"Sure. He was the one who wore his vest inside out."

"Pure stubbornness, that's what it was with Uncle Eb. He put it on inside out one day and someone laughed at him. So Uncle Eb said that was the way to wear a vest. And that's the way he wore it to his dying day."

"Well, sure," said Homer, "that might be it, of course. But wearing a vest inside out wouldn't hurt your chest. Shoes on the wrong feet would hurt something terrible."

"This poor Mr. Steen might be a cripple of some sort. Maybe he was born that way."

"I never heard of anyone born with his right and left feet switched."

"It's queer, naturally," Elaine persisted, "but what difference does it make? If you lease all those houses, we can go to

43

Europe like we've always planned. As far as I'm concerned, he can go barefoot if he wants."

"Yeah, I suppose so."

"And we need a car," Elaine said, beginning on her catalogue. "And drapes for the living room. And I haven't had a new dress in ages. And it's shameful to be using our old silver. We should have replaced it years ago. It's the old stuff Ethel gave us when we were married—"

"All right," said Homer. "If I lease the houses, if the deal holds up, if I don't get put in jail—we'll go to Europe."

He knew when he was licked.

He read the contract carefully. It was all right. It said, in black and white, that he got the whole five thousand.

Maybe, he told himself, he should have a lawyer see it. Al Congdon could tell him in a minute if it was ironclad. But he shrank from showing it. There seemed something sinful, almost shameful, about his getting all that money.

He checked on the Happy Acres Bank. A charter had been issued and all regulations had been met.

He checked on building permits and they were in order, too.

So what was a man to do?

Especially when he had a wife who had yearned loudly for ten years to go to Europe.

Homer sat down and wrote an ad for the real estate section of the Sunday paper. On second thought he dismissed the purple prose that he had planned to use. He employed the low-key technique. The ad wasn't long. It didn't cost too much. It read:

$4.16!!!!!
WOULD YOU PAY ONLY $4.16
a month to live in a house
that would sell for $35,000
to $50,000?
If so, call or see
JACKSON REAL ESTATE
*Specializing in Lake Property
and Country Acreages*

44

The first prospect was a man named H. F. Morgan. He came into the office early Sunday morning. He was belligerent. He slammed the folded want ad section down on Homer's desk. He had ringed Homer's ad with a big red-pencil mark.

"This isn't true!" yelled Morgan. "What kind of come-on is this?"

"It's substantially true," Homer answered quietly. "That's what it figures out to."

"You mean I just pay $4.16 a month?"

"Well," hedged Homer, "it's not quite as simple as all that. You lease it for ninety-nine years."

"What would I want with a house for ninety-nine years? I won't live that long."

"Actually, it's better than owning a house. You can live there a lifetime, just as if you owned the place, and there are no taxes and no maintenance. And if you have children, they can go on living there."

"You mean this is on the level?"

Homer emphatically nodded. "Absolutely."

"What's wrong with this house of yours?"

"There's nothing wrong with it. It's a new house among other new houses in an exclusive neighborhood. You have a shopping center just up the road that's as good as any city—"

"You say it's new?"

"Right. There are fifty houses. You can pick out the one you want. But I wouldn't take too long to decide, because these will go like hot cakes."

"I got my car outside."

"All right," said Homer, reaching for his hat. "I'll take my car and show you the way. The houses are unlocked. Look at them and choose the one you want."

Out on the street, Homer got into his car and sat down on something angular. He cursed because it hurt. He lifted himself and reached down and picked up the thing he'd sat on.

It was nothing he had ever seen before and he tossed it

45

to the other side of the seat. It was, he thought, something like one of those clip-together plastic blocks that were made for children, but how it had gotten in his car, he could not imagine.

He wheeled out into the street and signaled for the Morgan car to follow.

There were Mrs. Morgan and Jack, a hell-raising eight-year-old, and Judy, a winsome five-year-old, and Butch, the Boxer pup. All of them, Homer saw, were taken by surprise at the sight of Happy Acres. He could tell by the way Mrs. Morgan clasped her hands together and by the way suspicion darkened Morgan's face. One could almost hear him thinking that no one was crazy enough to offer a deal like this.

Jack and Butch, the pup, went running in the woods and Judy danced gaily on the lawn and, Homer told himself, he had them neatly hooked.

Homer spent a busy day. His phone was jammed with calls. House-hunting families, suspicious, half-derisive, descended on the office.

He did the best he could. He'd never had a crowd like this before.

He directed the house-hunting families out to Happy Acres. He patiently explained to callers that it was no hoax, that there were houses to be had. He urged all of them to hurry and make up their minds.

"They won't last long," he told them, intoning unctuously that most ancient of all real estate selling gimmicks.

After church, Elaine came down to the office to help him with the phone while he talked to the prospects who dropped in.

Late in the afternoon, he drove out to Happy Acres. The place was an utter madhouse. It looked like a homecoming or a state fair or a monster picnic. People were wandering around, walking through the houses. One had three windows broken. The floors were all tracked up. Water faucets had been left running. Someone had turned on a hose and washed out a flowerbed.

He tried to talk with some of them, but he made no headway. He went back to the office and waited for the rush to start.

There wasn't any rush.

A few phone calls came in and he assured the callers it was on the level. But they were still hard to convince.

He went home beat.

He hadn't leased a house.

Morgan was the first one who came back. He came back alone, early Monday morning. He was still suspicious.

"Look," he said, "I'm an architect. I know what houses cost. What's the catch?"

"The catch is that you pay five thousand cash for a ninety-nine-year lease."

"But that's no catch. That's like buying it. The normal house when it stands a hundred years, has long since lost its value."

"There's another catch," said Homer. "The builder won't lease to you unless you buy a new car from him."

"That's illegal!" shouted Morgan.

"I wouldn't know. Nobody's forcing you to take the offer."

"Let's forget about the car for the moment," Morgan urged. "What I want to know is, how can the builder put up a place like that for five thousand dollars? I know for a fact that he can't."

"So do I. But if he wants to lose a lot of money, who are we to stop him?"

Morgan pounded on the desk. "What's the gimmick, Jackson?"

"The builder wears his shoes on the wrong feet, if that means anything to you."

Morgan stared at him. "I think you're crazy, too. What would that have to do with it?"

"I don't know," said Homer. "I just mentioned it, thinking it might help you."

"Well, it doesn't."

Homer sighed. "It's got me puzzled, too."

Morgan picked up his hat and jammed it on his head. "I'll be seeing you," he said. It sounded like a threat.

"I'll be right here," said Homer as Morgan went slamming out the door.

Homer went down to the drugstore for a cup of coffee.

When he got back, a second visitor was waiting for him. The man sat stiffly in a chair and tapped nervous fingers on his briefcase, held primly in his lap. He looked as if he'd eaten something sour.

"Mr. Jackson," he said, "I represent the County Realtors Association."

"Not interested," said Homer. "I've gotten along for years without joining that outfit. I can get along a few years more."

"I'm not here to solicit membership. I am here about that ad of yours in the paper yesterday."

"Good ad, I thought. It brought in a lot of business."

"It's exactly the kind of advertising that our association frowns upon. It is, if you will pardon the expression, nothing but a come-on."

"Mr.—by the way, what is your name?"

"Snyder," said the man.

"Mr. Snyder, if you happen to be in the market for a place out in this area at the ridiculously low cost of $4.16 a month, I shall be glad to show you any one of fifty houses. If you have a moment, I can drive you out."

The man's mouth snapped together like a trap. "You know what I mean, Jackson. This is fraudulent advertising and you know it is. It is misrepresentation. We mean to show it is."

Homer pitched his hat on top of the filing cabinet and sat down in his chair.

"Snyder," he said, "you're cluttering up the place. You've done your duty—you've warned me. Now get out of here."

It wasn't exactly what he had meant to say and he was surprised at himself for saying it. But now that it was said, there was no way of recalling it and he rather liked the feel of strength and independence that it gave him.

"There is no use flying off the handle," said Snyder. "We could talk this over."

"You came in and made your threat," Homer retorted. "There's nothing to talk over. You said you were going to get me, so come ahead and get me."

Snyder got to his feet savagely. "You'll regret this, Jackson."

"Maybe so," admitted Homer. "Sure you don't need a house?"

"Not from you," said Snyder, and went stalking out.

Must have hurt their weekend sales, Homer told himself, watching Snyder go stumping down the street.

He sat quietly, thinking. He'd known there would be trouble, but there had been no way he could have passed up the deal. Not with Elaine set on that trip to Europe.

And now he was committed. He could not back out even if he wished. And he wasn't sure that he wanted to. There could be a lot of money in it.

The car deal he didn't like, but there was nothing he could do about it. And by handling it right, he might keep in the clear. Maybe, he thought, he should go out and talk to Steen about it.

Gabby Wilson, his insurance-selling neighbor down the hall, came in and flopped into a chair. Gabby was a loudmouth.

"Howsa boy?" he yelled. "Hear you got that Happy Acres deal. How's about cutting in your old pal on the insurance end?"

"Go chase yourself," invited Homer irritably.

"Heard a good story the other day. It seems this wrecking outfit got a job to tear down a building. And the straw boss got his orders wrong and tore down another building." Gabby slapped his knee and roared with laughter. "Can you imagine the look on that contractor's face when he heard the news?"

"It cost him a lot of money," Homer said. "He had a right to be good and sore."

"You don't think it's funny?"

"No, I don't."

"How you getting on with this Happy Acres gang?"

"Fine, so far," said Homer.

"Cheap outfit," Gabby told him. "I been checking round. They got some two-bit contractor from out in the sticks somewhere to do the job for them. Didn't even buy their material from the dealers here. The contractor brought his own crew with him. The developers didn't spend a nickel locally."

"Unpatriotic of them."

"Not smart, either. Houses probably will fall down in a year or two."

"I don't care particularly. Just so I get them leased."

"Do anything so far?"

"Got some interest in them. Here comes a prospect now."

It was Morgan. He had parked in front and was getting out of a new and shiny car, agleam with chrome.

Gabby beat a swift retreat.

Morgan came into the office. He sat down in a chair and pulled out his checkbook.

"I bought the car," he said. "How do you want this check made out?"

Six weeks later, Homer dropped in at the shopping center office. Steen was sitting with his feet up on the desk. He was wearing black shoes instead of the brown ones he had worn before. They still were on the wrong feet.

"Howdy, Mr. Jackson," he said easily.

Homer sat down in a chair. "I finally got rid of them. All the fifty houses are leased."

"That's fine." Steen reached into a drawer, took out a small book and tossed it across the desk to Homer. "Here. This belongs to you."

Homer picked it up. It was a bank book. He opened it

50

and saw a neat row of $4,500 entries marching down the page.

"You made yourself a mint," said Steen.

"I wish I had fifty more," Homer told him. "Or two hundred more. This thing is catching on. I could lease them in a week. I've got a waiting list longer than my arm."

"Well, why don't you go ahead and lease them?"

"I can't lease them a second time."

"Funny thing," said Steen. "There's no one living in those houses. They all are standing empty."

"But that can't be!" objected Homer. "There might be a few still empty—a few that the people haven't occupied yet. But most of them have moved in. They're living in those houses."

"That's not the way it looks to me."

"What's happened to those people then? Where have they—"

"Mr. Jackson!"

"Yes?"

"You haven't trusted me. You didn't trust me from the start. I don't know why. You thought the deal was queer. You were scared of it. But I've played fair with you. You'll have to admit I have."

Homer stroked the bank book. "More than fair."

"I know what I am doing, Mr. Jackson. I'm not anybody's fool. I have the angles figured out. String along with me. I need a man like you."

"You mean lease all those houses a *second* time!" Homer asked uneasily.

"A second time," said Steen. "And a third. And fourth. Lease them as often as you like. Keep right on leasing them. No one will mind at all."

"But the people will mind—the people that I lease those houses to," Homer pointed out.

"Mr. Jackson, let me handle this. Don't you worry about a solitary thing. You just keep those houses moving."

"But it isn't right."

"Mr. Jackson, in some six weeks' time, you've made a

51

quarter million dollars. I suppose that's what's wrong with you. I suppose you figure that's enough—"

"Well, no. With income tax and all—"

"Forget the income tax. I told you that this bank of ours had tax advantages."

"I don't get it," Homer said. "This is no way to do business."

"But it is," said Steen. "I challenge you to find a better way to do business. There's no end to it. You can become a multi-millionaire—"

"In jail."

"I've told you we weren't doing wrong. If you don't want to handle it—"

"Let me think it over," Homer pleaded. "Give me a day or two."

"Noon tomorrow," said Steen decisively. "If you don't tell me you are willing to go ahead by noon tomorrow, I'll look for someone else."

Homer got up. He thrust the bank book in his pocket. "I'll be in to see you."

Steen put his feet back on the desk. "Fine. I'll be expecting you."

Out on the concourse, Homer walked along the gleaming shop fronts. And the shops, he saw, were no more than half-staffed and entirely innocent of buyers. He went into a drugstore to buy a cigar and was waited on by a girl of just slightly more than high-school age. He failed to recognize her.

"You live around here?" he asked.

"No, sir. In the city."

He went into a hardware store and into a grocery supermarket. He saw no one he knew. And that was queer. He'd lived in the area for almost thirteen years and thought he knew everyone.

He recalled what Gabby had said about the contractor from somewhere out of town. Maybe, for some zany reason, Steen had a policy against employing local people. Still, he'd employed Homer.

It was a crazy setup, Homer told himself. None of it made sense—and least of all, the leasing of the houses a second time around.

Perhaps he should get out of it. He'd made a fair amount of money. Right now, most likely, he could get out slick and clean. If he stayed, there might be trouble.

He lighted up the cigar and went back to his car. Wheeling out of the parking lot, he headed for the road that led into the housing development.

He drove slowly, looking closely at each house. All of them seemed empty. The windows stared blindly without drapes or curtains. The lawns had not been cut for weeks. There was no sign of anyone—and there should be children and pets playing. Almost everyone he'd leased to had had children and dogs and cats. The place should be jumping, he told himself, and instead it was silent and deserted.

He stopped the car and went into a house. It was bare and empty. There was sawdust in the corners and wood shavings here and there. There were no scuff marks on the floor, no handprints on the wall. The windows had not been washed; the trade-mark paper still was sticking to them.

He went out puzzled.

He inspected two more houses. They were the same.

Steen had been right, then. Steen, with his shoes on the wrong feet, and with something else—with his different way of talking now. Six weeks ago, when Steen had come into Homer's office, he had been stiff and formal, awkward, yet striving for preciseness. And now he was easy in his manner, now he put his feet up on the desk, now he talked slangily.

There was no one living in the houses, Homer admitted to himself. No one had ever lived in them. He had leased all fifty of them and no one had moved in.

And it had a fishy smell—it had a terribly fishy smell.

On his way out, he stopped at Steen's office. The place was locked up.

53

The old gateman opened the gate and waved at him from the window of his kiosk.

Back in his own office, Homer took out of a drawer the list of leases he had drawn. He phoned Morgan, the first name on the lease.

"That number has been changed," the operator told him.

She gave him the new number and he dialed it.

"Happy Acres," said a singsong operator-voice.

"Huh?"

"Happy Acres," the voice sang. "Whom did you wish, sir?"

"The Morgan residence."

He waited and it was Morgan who answered.

"Homer Jackson. Just checking. How do you like the house? Are you getting on okay?"

"Perfectly," Morgan told him happily. "I've been meaning to come in and thank you for putting me onto this."

"Everything is really all right?"

"Couldn't be better. I hardly ever go into my office now. I stay out here and work in the amusement room. I go fishing and I take walks. The wife and kids are just as pleased as I am." Morgan lowered his voice. "How do you guys manage this? I've tried to figure it out and I can't."

"It's a secret," Homer replied, thinking on his feet. "The answer to the housing problem."

"Not that I care," Morgan said. "Just curious, you know. I'll be dropping in one day. I'll bring you something."

"Glad to see you," said Homer.

He called the Happy Acres number and asked for another family. He went halfway through the list. He talked mostly to the women, although some of the men were home. They were not only happy, but enthusiastic. They asked him jokingly how he got away with it.

When he finished, he was glassy-eyed.

He went down to the drugstore for a cup of coffee.

When he returned, he'd made up his mind.

54

He took out his waiting list and began making calls.

"There just happens to be a vacancy in Happy Acres if you are interested."

They were.

He reminded them about the cars. They said they'd take care of that matter first thing in the morning.

By suppertime, he'd leased twenty of the houses by making twenty phone calls.

"There's something wrong," Homer said to his wife. "But there's money in it."

"It's just that you don't understand," said Elaine. "There may be a perfectly good reason why Mr. Steen can't explain it all to you."

"But it means we have to give up our trip to Europe. And after we had got our passports and all."

"We can go to Europe later. You'll never get a chance like this again."

"It worries me," said Homer.

"Oh, you're always worried over things that never happen. Mr. Steen is satisfied and the people you have leased to are, so why are you worrying?"

"But where *are* these people? They aren't living in the houses and yet they talk as if they were. And some of them asked me how I got away with it or words to that effect. They asked it as if they admired me for being slick in some kind of shady deal, and if it turns out that I *am* smart, I'd like to know just how I managed—"

"Forget it," Elaine said. "You aren't smart and you never were. If I didn't keep behind you, pushing all the time—"

"Yes dear," said Homer. He'd heard it all before.

"And quit your worrying."

He tried to, but he couldn't.

The next morning, he drove to Happy Acres and parked across the road from the gate. From seven o'clock until nine, he counted forty-three cars coming out of the development. Some of the people in them he recognized as those he had leased the houses to. Many of them waved to him.

At 9:30, he drove in through the gate and went slowly down the road.

The houses still were empty.

When he got back to the office, there were people waiting for him. The block was clogged with cars that gleamed with newness.

He did a rushing business. No one, it turned out, was interested in seeing the houses. Most of them had seen them earlier. All they wanted was a lease. He filled out the forms as rapidly as he could and raked in the checks and cash.

Some other people showed up. Word had got around, they said, that there were vacancies in the Happy Acres tract. Yes, he said, there were. Just a few of them. He reminded them about the cars.

The last man in line, however, did not want to lease a house.

"My name is Fowler," he said. "I represent the Contractors and Builders Association. Maybe you can help me."

"I've got another house, if that is what you want," said Homer.

"I don't need a house. I have one, thanks."

"Pay you to sell it and get in on this deal. The newest thing in housing. A completely new concept."

Fowler shook his head. "All I want to know is, how do I get hold of Steen?"

"No trouble at all," said Homer. "You just go out to Happy Acres. He has an office there."

"I've been out there a dozen times. He is never in. Usually the office is locked."

"I never have any trouble finding him, although I don't see him often. I'm too busy handling the property."

"Can you tell me how he does it, Mr. Jackson?"

"How he does what? How he is always out?"

"No. How he can sell a house for five thousand dollars."

"He doesn't sell. He leases."

"Don't pull that one on me. It's the same as selling. And he can't build for anywhere near that kind of money. He's

56

losing a good twenty thousand or more on every house out there."

"If a man wants to lose his money—"

"Mr. Jackson," said Fowler, "that is not the point at all. The point is that it's unfair competition."

"Not if he leases," Homer pointed out. "If he sold, it might be."

"If this keeps on, it'll put every contractor in the area out of business."

"That," said Homer, "would be no more than simple justice in a lot of cases. They throw up a shack with plenty of glitter and charge a fancy price and—"

"Nevertheless, Mr. Jackson, none of them intend to be put out of business."

"And you're going to sue," guessed Homer.

"We certainly intend to."

"Don't look at me. I only lease the places."

"We intend to get out an injunction against your leasing them."

"You make the second one," Homer informed him, annoyed.

"The second what?"

"The real estate boys sent a guy like you out here several weeks ago. He made a lot of threats and nothing's happened yet. He was bluffing, just like you."

"Let me set your mind at rest," said Fowler. "I'm not doing any bluffing."

He got up from his chair and stalked stiffly out.

Homer looked at his watch. It was long past lunchtime. He went down to the drugstore for a sandwich and a cup of coffee. The place was empty and he had the counter to himself.

He sat hunched over the lunch and thought about it, trying to get all the queer goings-on straightened out into some sort of logic. But the only thing he could think about was that Steen wore his shoes on the wrong feet.

Wearily, still worried, Homer went back to the office.

There were people waiting, with their new cars parked outside. He leased houses right and left.

Apparently the word was spreading. The house-seekers drifted in all afternoon. He leased four more houses before it was time to close.

It was funny, he thought, very, very funny how the word had got around. He hadn't advertised in the last three weeks and they still were coming in.

Just as he was getting ready to lock up, Morgan strode in breezily. He had a package underneath his arm.

"Here you are, pal," he said. "I told you I'd bring you something. Caught them just an hour or two ago."

The package was beginning to get soggy. Homer took it gingerly.

"Thanks very much," he said in a doubtful voice.

"Think nothing of it. I'll bring you more in a week or two."

As soon as Morgan left, Homer closed the blinds and unwrapped the package warily.

Inside were brook trout—trout fresh-caught, with the ferns in which they had been wrapped not even wilting yet.

And there was no trout stream closer than a couple of hundred miles!

Homer stood and shivered. For there was no point in pretending ignorance, no point in repeating smugly to himself that it was all right. Even at five thousand a deal, there still was something wrong—very badly wrong.

He had to face it. They were beginning to close in on him. Fowler had sounded as if he might mean business and the Real Estate Association undoubtedly was lying in ambush, waiting for him to make one little slip. And when he made that slip, they'd snap the trap shut.

To protect himself, he had to know what was going on. He could no longer go at it blind.

Knowing, he might be able to go on. He might know when to quit. And that time, he told himself, might have been as early as this afternoon.

He stood there, with the fish and ferns lying in the wet

wrapping paper on the desk, and envisioned a long street of houses, and behind that long street of houses, another identical street of houses, and behind the second street, another—street after street, each behind the other, each exactly like the other, fading out of sight on a flat and level plain.

And that was the way it must be—except there was no second street of houses. There was just the one, standing lone and empty, and yet, somehow, with people living in them.

Lease them a second time, Steen had said, and a third time and a fourth. Don't you worry about a thing. Let me handle it. Leave the worry all to me. You just keep on leasing houses.

And Homer leased one house and the people moved, not into the house he'd leased them, but into the second identical house immediately behind it, and he leased the first house yet again and the people moved into the third, also identical, also directly behind the first and second house, and that was how it was.

Except it was just a childish thing he had dreamed up to offer an explanation—any explanation—for a thing he couldn't understand. A fairy tale.

He tried to get the idea back on the track again, tried to rationalize it, but it was too weird.

A man could trust his sense, couldn't he? He could believe what he could see. And there were only fifty houses— empty houses, despite the fact that people lived in them. He could trust his ears and he had talked to people who were enthusiastic about living in those empty houses.

It was crazy, Homer argued with himself. All those other folks were crazy—Steen and all the people living in the houses.

He wrapped up the fish and retied the package clumsily. No matter where they came from, no matter what lunacy might prevail, those trout surely would taste good. And that, the taste of fresh-caught trout, was one of the few true, solid things left in the entire world.

There was a creaking sound and Homer jumped in panic, whirling swiftly from the desk.

The door was being opened! He'd forgotten to lock the door!

The man who came in wore no uniform, but there was no doubt that he was a cop or detective.

"My name is Hankins," he said. He showed his badge to Homer.

Homer shut his mouth tight to keep his teeth from chattering.

"I think you may be able to do something for me," Hankins said.

"Surely," Homer chattered. "Anything you say."

"You know a man named Dahl?"

"I don't think I do."

"Would you search your records?"

"My records?" Homer echoed wildly.

"Mr. Jackson, you're a businessman. Surely you keep records—the names of persons to whom you sell property and other things like that."

"Yes," said Homer, all in a rush. "Yes, I keep that sort of record. Of course. Sure."

With shaking hands, he pulled out a desk drawer and brought out the folder he'd set up on Happy Acres. He looked through it, fumbling at the papers.

"I think I may have it," he said. "Dahl, did you say the name was?"

"John H. Dahl," said Hankins.

"Three weeks ago, I leased a house in Happy Acres to a John H. Dahl. Do you think he might be the one?"

"Tall, dark man. Forty-three years old. Acts nervous."

Homer shook his head. "I don't remember him. There have been so many people."

"Have you one there for Benny August?"

Homer searched again. "B. J. August. The day after Mr. Dahl."

"And perhaps a man named Drake? More than likely signs himself Hanson Drake."

Drake was also there.

Hankins seemed well pleased. "Now how do i get to this Happy Acres place?"

With a sinking feeling, Homer told him how.

He gathered up his fish and walked outside with Hankins. He stood and watched the officer drive away. He wouldn't want to be around, he suspected, when Hankins returned from Happy Acres. He hoped with all his heart that Hankins wouldn't look him up.

He locked up the office and went down to the drugstore to buy a paper before going home.

He unfolded it and the headlines leaped at him:

THREE HUNTED IN
STOCK SWINDLE

Three photographs on column cuts were ranged underneath the headline. He read the names in turn. Dahl. August. Drake.

He folded the paper tightly and thrust it beneath his arm and he felt the sweat begin to trickle.

Hankins would never find his men, he knew. No one would ever find them. In Happy Acres, they'd be safe. It was, he began to see, a ready-made hideout for all kinds of hunted men.

He wondered how many of the others he had leased the houses to might be hunted, too. No wonder, he thought, the word had spread so quickly. No wonder his office had been filled all day with people who'd already bought the cars.

And what was it all about? How did it work? Who had figured it all out?

And why did he, Homer Jackson, have to be the one who'd get sucked into it?

Elaine took a searching look at him as he came in the door.

"You've been worrying," she scolded.

Homer lied most nobly. "Not worrying. Just a little tired."

"Scared to death" would have been closer to the truth.

At 9 o'clock next morning, he drove to Happy Acres. He was inside the door before he saw that Steen was busy. The man who had been talking to Steen swung swiftly from the desk.

"Oh, it's you," he said.

Homer saw that the man was Hankins.

Steen smiled wearily. "Mr. Hankins seems to think that we're obstructing justice."

"I can't imagine," Homer said, "why he should think that."

Hankins was on the edge of rage. "Where are these people? What have you done with them?"

Steen said: "I've told you, Mr. Hankins, that we only lease the property. We cannot undertake to go surety for anybody who may lease from us."

"You've hidden them!"

"How could we hide them, Mr. Hankins? *Where* could we hide them? The entire development is open to you. You can search it to your heart's content."

"I don't know what is going on," said Hankins savagely, "but I'm going to find out. And once I do, both of you had better have your explanations ready."

"I think," Steen commented, "that Mr. Hankins' determination and deep sense of duty are very splendid things. Don't you, Mr. Jackson?"

"I do, indeed," said Homer, at loss as to what to say.

"You'll be saying that out of the other side of your mouth before I'm through with you," Hankins promised them.

He went storming out the door.

"What a nasty man," Steen remarked, unconcerned.

"I'm getting out," said Homer. "I've got a pocket full of checks and cash. As soon as I turn them over, I am pulling out. You can find someone else to do your dirty work."

"Now I am sorry to hear that. And just when you were doing well. There's a lot of money to be made."

"It's too risky."

"I grant you that it may appear a little risky, but actually it's not. Men like Hankins will raise a lot of dust, but what can they really do? We are completely in the clear."

"We're leasing the same houses over and over again."

"Why, certainly," said Steen. "How else would you expect me to build up the kind of clientele I need to give me business volume in this shopping center? You yourself have told me that fifty families were by no means enough. And you were right, of course. But you lease the houses ten times and you have five hundred families, which is not bad. Lease each one a hundred times and you have five thousand— And incidentally, Mr. Jackson, by the time you lease each of them a hundred times, you will have made yourself twenty-five million dollars, which is not a bad amount for a few years' work.

"Because," Steen concluded, "you see, despite what you may have thought of me, I'm squarely on the level. I gave you the straight goods. I told you I was not interested in money from the houses, but merely from the shopping center."

Homer tried to pretend that he was unimpressed. He kept on emptying checks and wads of money from his pockets. Steen reached out for the checks and began endorsing them. He stacked the money neatly.

"I wish you would reconsider, Mr. Jackson," he urged. "I have need of a man like you. You've worked out so satisfactorily, I hate to see you go."

"Come clean with me," said Homer, "and I might stay. Tell me all there is to tell—how it all works and what all the angles are and what you plan to do."

Steen laid a cautionary finger across his lips. "Hush! You don't know what you're asking."

"You mean you see no trouble coming?"

"Some annoyance, perhaps. Not real trouble."

"They could throw the book at us if they could prove we were hiding people wanted by the law."

Steen sighed deeply. "Mr. Jackson, how many fugitives have you sheltered in the last six weeks?"

"Not a one," said Homer.

"Neither have I." Steen spread his arms wide. "So we have nothing to fear. We've done no wrong. At least," he amended, "none that they can prove."

He picked up the money and the checks and handed them to Homer.

"Here," he said. "You might as well take it to the bank. It's your money."

Homer took the money and the checks and stood with them in his hand, thinking about what Steen had said about not doing any wrong. Maybe Steen was right. Maybe Homer was getting scared when there was no need to be.

What could they be charged with?

Fraudulent advertising? There had been no specific claims that had not been performed.

For tying in the auto sales? Just possibly, although he had not made an auto sale a condition of transaction; he had merely mentioned that it would be very nice if they bought a car from Happy Acres Auto Sales.

For selling at less than cost? Probably not, for it would be a fine point of law to prove a lease a sale. And selling or leasing below cost in any case was no crime.

For leasing the same house more than once? Certainly not until it could be proved that someone had suffered damage and it was most unlikely that it could be proved.

For doing away with people? But those people could be reached by telephone, could drive out through the gate. And they were well and happy and enthusiastic.

"Perhaps," Steen said gently, "you have changed your mind. Perhaps you'll stay with us."

"Perhaps I will," said Homer.

He walked down the concourse to the bank. It was an impressive place. The foyer was resplendent in coppery metal and with brightly polished mirrors. There were birds in hanging cages and some of the birds were singing.

There were no customers, but the bank was spic and span. An alert vice-president sat behind his polished desk without a thing to do. An equally alert teller waited shiny-faced behind the wicket window.

Homer walked to the window and shoved through the money and the checks. He took his passbook from his pocket and handed it across.

The teller looked at it and said, "I'm sorry, Mr. Jackson, but you have no account with us."

"No account!" cried Homer. "I have a quarter of a million!"

His heart went plunk into his boots, and if he'd had Steen there, he'd have broken him to bits.

"No," said the teller calmly, "you've made an error. That is all."

"Error!" gasped Homer, hanging onto the window to keep from keeling over.

"An understandable error," the teller said sympathetically. "One that anyone could make. Your account is not with us, but with the Second Bank."

"Second Bank," wheezed Homer. "What are you talking about? This is the only bank there is."

"Look, it says *Second Bank* right here." He showed Homer the passbook. It did say *Second Happy Acres State Bank*.

"Well, now," said Homer, "that's better. Will you tell me how I get to this Second Bank?"

"Gladly, sir. Right over there. Just go through that door."

He handed back the passbook and the money.

"That door, you say?" inquired Homer.

"Yes. The one beside the drinking fountain."

Homer clutched the passbook and the money tightly in his hand and headed for the door. He opened it and stepped inside and got it shut behind him before he realized that he was in a closet.

It was just a tiny place, not much bigger than a man, and it was as black as the inside of a cat.

Sweat started out on Homer and he searched frantically for the doorknob and finally found it.

He pushed the door open and stumbled out. He strode wrathfully back across the foyer to the teller's window. He rapped angrily on the ledge and the teller turned around.

"What kind of trick is this?" yelled Homer. "What do you think you're pulling? What is going on here? That is nothing but a closet."

"I'm sorry, sir," the teller said. "My fault. I forgot to give you this."

He reached into his cash drawer and handed Homer a small object. It looked for all the world like the replica of a bizarre radiator ornament.

Juggling the object in his hand, Homer asked, "What has this got to do with it?"

"Everything," the teller said. "It will get you to the Second Bank. Don't lose it. You'll need it to get back."

"You mean I just hold it in my hand?"

"That is all you do, sir," the teller assured him.

Homer went back to the door, still unconvinced. It was all a lot of mumbo-jumbo, he told himself. These guys were just the same as Gabby Wilson—full of smart pranks. And if that teller was making a fool of him, he promised himself, he'd mop up the floor with him.

He opened the door and stepped into the closet, only it was no closet. It was another bank.

The metal still was coppery and the mirrors were a-glitter and the birds were singing, but there were customers. There were three tellers instead of the single one in the first bank and the bland, smooth vice-president at his shiny desk was industriously at work.

Homer stood quietly just outside the door through which he'd come from the other bank. The customers seemed not to have noticed him, but as he looked them over, he was startled to discover that there were many whose faces were familiar.

Here, then, were the people who had leased the houses, going about their business in the Second Bank.

He put the miniature radiator ornament in his pocket and headed for the window that seemed to be least busy. He waited in line while the man ahead of him finished making a deposit.

Homer could only see the back of the man's head, but the head seemed to be familiar. He stood there raking through the memories of the people he had met in the last six weeks.

Then the man turned around and Homer saw that it was Dahl. It was the same face he had seen staring at him from the front page of the paper only the night before.

"Hello, Mr. Jackson," said Dahl. "Long time no see."

Homer gulped. "Good day, Mr. Dahl. How do you like the house?"

"Just great, Mr. Jackson. It's so quiet and peaceful here, I can't tear myself away from it."

I bet you can't, thought Homer.

"Glad to hear you say so," he said aloud, and stepped up to the window.

The teller glanced at the passbook. "Good to see you, Mr. Jackson. The president, I think, would like to see you, too. Would you care to step around after I finish your deposit?"

Homer left the teller's window, feeling a little chilly at the prospect of seeing the president, wondering what the president might want and what new trouble it portended.

A hearty voice told him to come in when he knocked on the door.

The president was a beefy gentleman and extremely pleasant.

"I've been hoping you'd come in," he said. "I don't know if you realize it or not, but you're our biggest depositor."

He shook Homer's hand most cordially and motioned him to a chair. He gave him a cigar and Homer, a good judge of tobacco, figured it for at least a fifty-center.

The president, puffing a little, sat down behind his desk.

"This is a good setup here," said Homer, to get the conversation started.

"Oh, yes," the president said. "Most splendid. It's just a test, though, you know."

"No, I hadn't known that."

"Yes, surely. To see if it will work. If it does, we will embark on much bigger projects—ones that will prove even more economically feasible. One never knows, of course, how an idea will catch on. You can run all the preliminary observations and make innumerable surveys and still never know until you try it out."

"That's true," said Homer, wondering what in the world the president was talking about.

"Once we get it all worked out," the president said, "we can turn it over to the natives."

"I see. You're not a native here?"

"Of course not. I am from the city."

And that, thought Homer, was a funny thing to say. He watched the man closely, but there was nothing in his face to indicate that he had misspoken—no flush of embarrassment, no sign of flurry.

"I'm especially glad to have a chance to see you," Homer told him. "As a matter of fact, I had been thinking of switching my account and—"

The president's face took on a look of horror. "But why? Certainly you've been told about the tax advantages."

"I think that the matter got some mention. But, I must confess, I don't understand."

"Why, Mr. Jackson, it is simple. No mystery at all. So far as the authorities of your country are concerned—"

"My country?"

"Well, of course. I think it might logically be argued, even in a court of law, that this place we're in is no longer the United States of America. But even if it should be a part of your great nation—I doubt that such a contention would hold up if put to the decision—why, even so, our records are not available to the agents of your country.

Don't tell me you fail to see the implications of a situation such as that."

"The income tax," Homer said.

"Correct," said the president, smiling very blandly.

"That is interesting. Interesting, indeed." Homer rose and held out his hand to the president. "I'll be in again."

"Thank you," said the president. "Drop in any time you wish."

On the street outside the bank, the sun was shining brightly. The shopping center stretched along the mall and there were people here and there, walking on the concourse or shopping in the stores. A few cars were parked in the lot and the world of this Second Bank looked exactly like the First Bank's world, and if a man had not known the difference—

Good Lord, thought Homer, what *was* the difference? What had really happened? He'd walked through the door and there was the other bank. He'd walked through a door and found the missing people—the people who had not been living in the empty houses of the First Bank's world.

Because that other world where the houses still stood empty was no more than a show window? It might simply be a street lined with demonstration homes. And here was that second street of houses he'd dreamed up the other night. And beyond this second street, would there be another street and another and another?

He stumbled along the concourse, shaken, now that he realized there really was that second street of houses. It was an idea that was hard to take in stride. He didn't take it in his stride. His mind balked and shied away from it and he told himself it wasn't true. But it was true and there was no way to rationalize it, to make it go away.

There *was* a second street!

He walked along and saw that he was near the gate. The gate, he saw, was the same as ever, with its expanse of massive iron. But there was no gateman.

And a car was coming up the road, heading directly for

69

the gate, and it was moving fast, as if the driver did not see the gate.

Homer shouted and the car kept on. He started to run, waving his arms, but the driver paid not the least attention.

The crazy fool, thought Homer. He'll hit the gate and—

And the car hit the gate, slammed into it, but there was no sound, no crash, no screech of rending metal. There was simply nothing.

The gate was there, undented. And there was no car. The car had disappeared.

Homer stalked to the gate.

Ten feet away, he stopped.

The road came up to the gate; beyond it was no road. Beyond the gate was wilderness. The road came up and ended and the wilderness began.

Cautiously, Homer walked out into the road and peered through the gate.

Just a few feet away, a giant oak towered into the air and behind it was the forest, wild and hoary and primeval, and in the forest was the happy sound, the abandoned sound of water running in a brook.

Fish, thought Homer. Maybe that brook is where the trout came from.

He moved toward the gate for a closer look and reached out his hands to grasp the ironwork. Even as he did, the forest went away and the gate as well as he stood in the old familiar entrance to Happy Acres, with the gate wide open, with the state highway running along the wall and the road from the development running out to meet it.

"Good morning, sir," said the gateman. "Maybe you ought to move over to one side. A car is apt to hit you."

"Huh?" Homer asked blankly.

"A car. This is a road, you know."

Homer turned around and brushed past the gateman. He hustled down the concourse, aiming for Steen's office.

But the office was locked. Homer shook the door. He

rapped wildly on the glass. He pounded on the frame. Absolutely nothing happened.

Turning from the door, he stared out across the development with incredulous eyes—the vacant concourse, the empty houses among the trees, the faint patches of shining lake peeking through the clearings.

He jammed his hands into his pockets and his fingers touched the little radiator ornament. He took it out and looked at it. He'd seen it before—not the little replica, but the ornament itself.

He had seen it, he remembered, on the new cars parked outside his office by the people seeking leases. He had seen it on the car that had crashed the gate and disappeared.

He walked slowly to the parking lot and drove home.

"I don't think I'll go back to the office today," he told Elaine. "I don't feel so good."

"You've been working too hard," she told him accusingly. "You look all worn out."

"That's a fact," he admitted.

"After lunch, you lie down. And see that you get some sleep."

"Yes, dear," he said.

So it began to fall into a pattern, he thought, lying on his bed and staring at the ceiling. Finally it was clear enough so a man could begin to make some head and tail of it.

It was unbelievable, but there was no choice—one could not disbelieve in it. It was there to see. And if one looked at it any other way, it made no sense at all.

Someone—Steen, perhaps, or maybe someone else for whom Steen was serving as a front—had found out how to build one house, yet have many houses, houses stretching back street after street from the first house, all shadows of the first house, but substantial just the same—substantial enough for families to live in.

Dimensional extensions of that first house. Or houses stretching into time. Or something else as weird.

71

But however they might do it, it was a swell idea. For you could build one house and sell it, or lease it, time and time again. Except that one was crazy to get hold of an idea that was as good as that and then let someone else make all the money from the leasing of the houses.

And there was no question that Steen was crazy. That idea he had about the shopping center was completely batty—although, stop to think of it, if one had five thousand houses and leased each of them ten times and had a monopoly on all the shops and stores—why, it would pay off tremendously.

And the bank president's slant on sovereignty had certain angles, too, that should not be overlooked.

A new idea in housing, Steen had told him. It was all of that. It was a new idea that would apply to many things—to industry and farming and mining and a lot of other ventures. A man could make one car and there would be many others. A man could build a manufacturing plant and he would have many plants.

It was like a carbon copy, Homer thought—an economic carbon copy. And a man apparently could make as many carbons as he wished. Possibly, he speculated, once you knew the principle, there was no limit to the carbons. Possibly the ghostly parade of Happy Acres houses stretched limitless, forever and forever. There might be no end to them.

He fell asleep and dreamed of going down a line of ghostly houses, counting them frantically as he ran along, hoping that he'd soon get to the end of them, for he couldn't quit until he did get to the end. But they always stretched ahead of him, as far as he could see, and he could find no end to them.

He woke, damp with perspiration, his tongue a dry and bitter wad inside a flannel mouth. He crept out of bed and went to the bathroom. He held his head under a cold faucet. It helped, but not much.

Downstairs, he found a note that Elaine had propped

against the radio on the breakfast table: *Gone to play bridge at Mabel's. Sandwiches in refrigerator.*

It was dark outside. He'd slept the daylight hours away. A wasted day, he berated himself—a completely wasted day. He hadn't done a dollar's worth of work.

He found some milk and drank it, but left the sandwiches where they were.

He might as well go to the office and get a little work done, compensate in part for the wasted day. Elaine wouldn't return until almost midnight and there was no sense in staying home alone.

He got his hat and went out to where he'd parked the car in the driveway. He got into it and sat down on something angular and hard. He hoisted himself wrathfully and searched the seat with a groping hand to find the thing he'd sat on.

His fingers closed about it and then he remembered. He'd sat on it on that day Morgan had showed up in answer to the ad. It had been rolling around ever since, unnoticed in the seat.

It was smooth to the touch and warm—warmer than it should be—as if there were a busy little motor humming away inside it.

And suddenly it winked.

He caught his breath and it flashed again.

Exactly like a signal.

Instinct told him to get rid of it, to heave it out the window, but a voice suddenly spoke out of it—a thick, harsh voice that mouthed a sort of chant he could not recognize.

"What the hell?" chattered Homer, fearful now. "What's going on?"

The chanting voice ceased and a heavy silence fell, so thick and frightening that Homer imagined he could feel it closing in on him.

The voice spoke again. This time, it was one word, slow and labored, as if the thick, harsh tongue drove itself to create a new and alien sound.

The silence fell again and there was a sense of waiting. Homer huddled in the seat, cold with fear.

For now he could guess where the cube had come from. Steen had ridden in the car with him and it had fallen from his pocket.

The voice took up again: "Urrr—urr—urrth—mum!"

Homer almost screamed.

Rustling, panting sounds whispered from the cube.

Earthman? Homer wondered wildly. Was that what it had tried to say?

And if that was right, if the cube in fact had been lost by Steen, then it meant that Steen was not a man at all.

He thought of Steen and the way he wore his shoes and suddenly it became understandable why he might wear his shoes that way. Perhaps, where Steen came from, there was no left or right, maybe not even shoes. No man could expect an alien, a being from some distant star, to get the hang of all Earth's customs—not right away, at least. He recalled the first day Steen had come into the office and the precise way he had talked and how stiffly he'd sat down in the chair. And that other day, six weeks later, when Steen had talked slangily and had sat slouched in his chair, with his feet planted on the desk.

Learning, Homer thought. Learning all the time. Getting to know his way around, getting the feel of things, like a gawky country youth learning city ways.

But it sure was a funny thing that he'd never learned about the shoes.

The cube went on gurgling and panting and the thick voice muttered and spat out alien words. One could sense the tenseness and confusion at the other end.

Homer sat cold and rigid, with horror seeping into him drop by splashing drop, while the cube blurted over and over a single phrase that meant not a thing to him.

Then, abruptly, the cube went dead. It lay within his hand, cooling, silent, just a thing that looked and felt like a clip-together plastic block for children.

From far off, he heard the roar of a car as it left the

curb and sped off in the night. From someone's backyard, a cat meowed for attention. Nearby, a bird cheeped sleepily.

Homer opened the glove compartment and tossed the cube in among the rags and scraper and the dog-eared roadmap and the other odds and ends.

He felt the terror and the loathing and the wild agony begin to drain out of his bones and he sat quietly in the car, trying to readjust his mind to this new situation—that Steen must be an alien.

He dipped his hand into his pocket and found the replica of the radiator ornament. And that was the key, he knew— not only the key to the many streets of homes, but the key to Steen and the alien world.

They hadn't meant for him to keep the ornament, of course. If he had returned the way he'd entered the world of the Second Bank, the teller more than likely would have demanded that he give it back. But he'd returned another way, an unexpected way, and it still was in his pocket.

And the radiator ornament, of course, was the reason that Steen had insisted that anyone who leased a house must also buy a car. For the ornament was a key that bridged one world and another. Although, thought Homer, it was rather drastic to insist that a man should buy a car simply so he'd have the correct radiator ornament.

But that might be the way, he told himself, that an alien mind would work.

He was calmer now. The fear still lingered, but pushed back, buried just a little.

Exactly how is a man supposed to act, he asked himself, when he learns there are aliens in the land? Run screeching through the streets, rouse all the citizens, alert the law, go baying on the trail? Or does he continue about his business?

Might he not, he wondered, take advantage of his knowledge, turn it to his own benefit?

He was the only human being on all of Earth who knew. Steen might not like it known that he was an alien. Perhaps it would be worth a lot to Steen not to have it known.

Homer sat and thought about it. The more he thought, the more reasonable it seemed that Steen might be ready to lay plenty on the line to keep the fact a secret.

Not that I don't have it coming to me, Homer told himself. Not that he hasn't caused me a heap of worry and trouble.

He put his hand into his pocket. The miniature ornament was there. There was no need to wait. Now was as good as any time.

He turned the ignition key and the motor came to life. He backed out of the driveway and took the road to Happy Acres.

The development was dark and quiet. Even the usual advertising signs were turned off in the shop fronts.

He parked in front of Steen's office and got out. Opening the trunk, he found the jack handle in the dark.

He stood staring toward the gate. There was no sign of the gateman. But that was a chance he'd have to take. If the old fool tried to interfere, he could handle him.

For a moment, in front of the door to Steen's office, he hesitated, trying to reassure himself. Certainly there would be another closet, some way to get to those other worlds, inside the office.

He struck savagely at the glass in the door with the jack handle. The glass splintered and rained down, with crashing, tinkling sounds.

Homer waited, tense, listening, watching. Nothing stirred. The old gateman, if he was around, apparently had not heard the crash.

Carefully, Homer reached through the broken glass and manipulated the night lock. The door swung easily open. He walked inside and closed the door behind him.

In the empty office, Homer paused until his eyes became accustomed to the deeper darkness. He moved forward, groping with his hands, and found the desk. He could make out the dim bulk of a filing case. There should be a door somewhere. Perhaps not a door into the street, but a

76

door into a hideout—some room where Steen could disappear to eat and rest and sleep; some place that might have a touch of his alien home about it.

Homer moved from the desk to the filing cabinet and felt along the wall. Almost immediately, he found a door.

He took a firmer grip on the jack handle and twisted on the knob. He walked through the door and there was the room, lighted a garish green by a lantern suspended from the ceiling.

There was sound and the sense of movement. Homer's hair stood straight on end and he felt his skin trying very hard to roll up his back. The hairy monster reached out a paw and grabbed him by the shoulder just as Homer swung around to dive back through the door.

The monster's paw was heavy and very strong. It was hairy and it tickled. Homer opened his mouth to scream, but his tongue dried up and his throat closed and he couldn't make a sound. The jack handle slipped from his numb fingers and clattered to the floor.

For a long moment, he stood there in the grip of the hairy monster and he supposed it had a face, but he could not see the face, for the hair grew all over it and drooped down where its face should be. The monster was a large one, with massive chest and shoulders that tapered down to a slim, athletic waist. Frightened as he was, Homer still could not keep from thinking that it looked a lot like an English sheepdog with a wrestler's body.

And all the while, there was something rolling on the floor and moaning.

Then the hairy monster said, in halting, stumbling syllables: "You Mister Jackson, you are not?"

Homer made a croaking sound.

"I apologize," the monster told him. "I very poor at your words. I work on your planet survey, but not so good with words."

He motioned at the thing moaning and rolling on the floor. "That was good with words."

The hairy hand dropped from Homer's shoulder.

"That," it said, gesturing at the floor again, "your Mister Steen."

"What is wrong with him?" Homer blurted out. "Is he sick or something?"

"He die himself," the monster said.

"You mean he's dying and you're just standing there—"

"No, no. He—how do you word it right?—he unlive himself."

"You mean he's killing himself? Committing suicide?"

"Yes," the monster said. "He does it very well. Do you not agree?"

"But you can't—"

"He take great pride in it. He make spectacular. He just starting now. He work up to grand finale. You must stay and watch. It be something to remember."

"No, thank you," Homer said faintly.

Homer turned to go, but the monster put out a hairy paw and stopped him.

"You must not be afraid of us. I stay half myself, all right? Could change entirely into human, but much trouble. Good enough this way?"

"It's all right," said Homer.

"We owe you debt," the monster said. "This Mister Steen of yours got things all scrambled up."

"I'll say he did," said Homer feelingly.

"He just a stumblebum. Bungler. He likewise is a joker."

"Joker?"

"Clown? Wise guy? You know—he made the joke. Sometimes very sly joke, but stupid just the same."

The monster leaned forward to peer into Homer's face.

"Your planet, it has its jokers, too?"

"Yes, indeed," Homer said. "There's one down the hall from me. His name is Gabby Wilson."

"So you understand then. A joker not too bad if that is all he is. But take a joker who makes mistakes and that is most bad. You have name for it. Smart aleck?"

"That's the name," said Homer.

"We make projects for the planets, for very many planets.

78

We try to make each project fit the planet. The kind that will help the planet, the kind it needs the most."

"Like foreign aid," Homer supplied.

"So this bungler," said the monster, his voice rising in forthright and honest wrath, "this smart aleck, this nincompoop, this Mister Steen of yours, what do you think he does? He came to Earth as project manager—and he brings *wrong plan!* He is like that other times, going off not cocked. But this, it is too much. Final straw."

"You mean this Happy Acres business was never meant for Earth, but for some other planet?"

The monster draped his arm around Homer's shoulder in a gesture of understanding and affection. "That exactly what he do. No need of Happy Acres here. You still have room enough for all your people. No need to double up."

"But, sir," said Homer earnestly, "it is a swell idea. It has possibilities."

"Other things you need much worse, my friend. We have better plan for you."

Homer couldn't decide whether he liked the way the monster talked about the better plan.

"What other plan?" he asked.

"That is topmost secret. To make project big success, it must be done so that the natives think they the ones who do it. And that," the monster said, gesturing toward the floor, "is where this silly obscenity failed in second place. He let you find out what was going on."

"But there were all the other people, too," Homer protested. "All the people in the shops. The bank president and the gateman and—"

"All of them is us," the monster explained. "Them the crew that came with Mister Steen."

"But they were so human-looking! They looked exactly like us!"

"They play it straight, This ape, he ham it up."

"But they dressed like us and they wore shoes—"

"The shoes was more joke," the monster said furiously. "Your Mister Steen, he know how to make himself a human like the rest of them. But he wear his shoes wrong to get you humans—your humans'—there is a word for it."

"Goat?"

"That is it! He wear them wrong to get your humans' goat. And he make outrageous deal with you and he watch you worry and he rejoice greatly and think himself superior and smart because he that kind of clown. That, I tell you, is no way to treat anyone. That is no true-blue friendship. But your Mister Steen, he was plain jerk. Let us go and watch him suffer."

"No," said Homer, horrified.

"You no like this dying?"

"It's inhuman."

"Of course, inhuman. We not humans, us. It is a way we have, a social law. He make himself a fool. He make bone-head blunder. He must dead himself. He must do it good. Great honor, do it good. He bungle everything in life, he must not bungle dying. He forever heel if he do."

Homer shivered, listening to the anguish of the alien on the floor, sick at stomach and giddy in the green flood of alien light.

"Now it is to end," said the alien. "We wipe out project. It was nonsensical mistake. We will take it all away."

"You can't mean that!" argued Homer. "We need it. We could make use of it. Just show us the principle."

"No," the monster said.

"But if you wipe out the project, there'll be all these people—"

"Sorry."

"They'll murder me! I was the one who leased the houses to them—"

"Too bad," the monster said.

"And all that money in the bank! A quarter of a million dollars, more than a quarter of a million dollars! It will be wiped out!"

"You have human money in bank?"

"I did. I suppose *that's* too bad, too."

80

"We can pay you off. Mister Steen make a lot of money. He store it over there."

He pointed to the far wall. "You see that pile of bags? You take all that you can carry."

"Money?" Homer asked.

"Good money."

"All I can carry?" insisted Homer, nailing it down tight. "And you will let me leave?' '

"We do you wrong," the monster said. "This fix it just a little?"

"I'll tell the world," said Homer, with enthusiasm.

Steen was becoming noisier. He had changed into his alien form and now he rolled upon the floor, knotted up and writhing.

Homer walked wide around him to get to the farther wall. He lifted down the bags and they were fairly heavy. He could take two at least, he figured. He hoisted two on his back, then piled on the third. He barely made it back across the room.

The monster watched him with some admiration. "You like money, huh?"

"You bet," Homer panted. "Everyone likes money."

He set the bags down by the door.

"You sure you not stay and watch? It get good directly. It be amusing, maybe even interesting."

Homer held down a rising shudder. "No, thank you very much."

The monster helped him get the bags on his shoulder. "I hold the door for you."

"Thank you," said Homer. "Good day to you and thanks for everything."

"Good-by, my friend," the monster said.

He held the door and Homer walked on through.

He came back into the office he'd left an hour before, the glass in the door shattered and his car still parked outside.

Homer hurried.

In less than five minutes, he went roaring out the gate, with the bags of money locked inside the trunk.

There was little time, he realized. What he did had to be done fast. For when the monster wiped out Happy Acres, there would be a battalion of families marooned there in the woods and they'd come boiling out with a single thought in mind—to get their hands on Homer Jackson.

He tried to imagine what it might be like, and then tried to stop thinking what it might be like, but couldn't.

There would be a lot of people there without any houses. They'd wake up in the wild, wet woods with their furniture and belongings scattered all about them. And all those bright new cars would be in among the trees. And the people would be plenty sore.

Not that he blamed them much.

He was sore himself.

That lousy Steen, he said. Like that contractor Gabby told about—the one who went out on a wrecking job and demolished the wrong house.

The dashboard clock said slightly after midnight. Elaine would be home by now and they could start right out.

Homer turned into the driveway and braked to a halt. There was a light in the kitchen window. He ran up the walk and burst into the house.

"Oh, *there* you are," said Elaine. "I wondered where you were. What's wrong with you?"

"We're getting out of here," Homer babbled.

"Have you gone stark crazy? Getting out!"

"Now for once," said Homer, "don't give me an argument. We're getting out of here. Tonight. I've got three sacks of money out there in the car—"

"Money! How did you get three sacks—"

"It's legal," Homer pleaded. "There's nothing wrong with it. I didn't rob a bank. There's no time to explain. Let us just get going."

She got icy calm. "Where are we going, Homer?"

"We can decide that later. Maybe Mexico."

"You're ill," she scolded. "You've been working too hard lately. And worrying about that Happy Acres deal—"

It was too much for Homer. He turned toward the door.

"Homer! Where are you going, Homer!"

"I'll show you the money," he gritted. "I'll show you I really have it."

"Wait for me," she cried, but he didn't wait. She ran down the walk behind him.

He opened the car trunk. "There it is. We'll carry it up to the house. You can take off your shoes and walk in it. Then maybe you'll believe me."

"No, Homer, no!"

"Here, help me with these sacks," he said.

Inside the house, he opened the sacks. Neatly bundled sheafs of bills spilled out on the floor.

Elaine knelt and picked up a package.

"Why, it's real!" she cried happily.

"Of course it is," said Homer.

"And, Homer, these are twenty-thousand-dollar bills!"

She dropped the package that she held and picked up another and another and another.

"And so are these!" she screamed. "There are millions and millions here!"

Homer was pawing desperately through the heap of money. Sweat was running down his face.

"Are they all twenty-thousand-dollar bills?" she asked hopefully.

"Yes," said Homer in a beaten voice.

"But what is wrong?"

"That dirty, lowdown, bungling Steen," he said bitterly.

"But what is wrong?" she cried again.

"They aren't worth a dime," said Homer. "There are no such things as twenty-thousand-dollar bills. The Treasury never issued any!"

Founding Father

WINSTON-KIRBY WALKED HOME across the moor just before the twilight hour and it was then, he felt, that the land was at its best. The sun was sinking into a crimson froth of clouds and the first gray-silver light began to run across the swales. There were moments when it seemed all eternity grew quiet and watched with held breath.

It had been a good day and it would be a good homecoming, for the others would be waiting for him with the dinner table set and the fireplace blazing and the drinks set close at hand. It was a pity, he thought, that they would not go walking with him, although, in this particular instance, he was rather glad they hadn't. Once in a while, it was a good thing for a man to be alone. For almost a hundred years, aboard the ship, there had been no chance to be alone.

But that was over now and they could settle down, just the six of them, to lead the kind of life they'd planned. After only a few short weeks, the planet was beginning to seem like home; in the years to come, it would become in truth a home such as Earth had never been.

Once again he felt the twinge of recurring wonder at how they'd ever got away with it. That Earth should allow six of its immortals to slip through its clutches seemed unbelievable. Earth had real and urgent need for all of its immortals, and that not one, but six, of them should be allowed to slip away, to live lives of their own, was beyond all logic. And yet that was exactly what had happened.

There was something queer about it, Winston-Kirby told

himself. On the century-long flight from Earth, they'd often talked about it and wondered how it had come about. Cranford-Adams, he recalled, had been convinced that it was some subtle trap, but after a hundred years there was no evidence of any trap and it had begun to seem Cranford-Adams must be wrong.

Winston-Kirby topped the gentle rise that he had been climbing and, in the gathering dusk, he saw the manor house—exactly the kind of house he had dreamed about for years, precisely the kind of house to be built in such a setting—except that the robots had built it much too large. But that, he consoled himself, was what one had to expect of robots. Efficient, certainly, and very well intentioned and obedient and nice to have around, but sometimes pretty stupid.

He stood on the hilltop and gazed down upon the house. How many times had he and his companions, at the dinner table, planned the kind of house they would build? How often had they speculated upon the accuracy of the specifications given for this planet they had chosen from the Exploratory Files, fearful that it might not be in every actuality the way it was described?

But here, finally, it was—something out of Hardy, something from the Baskervilles—the long imagining come to comfortable reality.

There was the manor house, with the light shining from its windows, and the dark bulk of the outbuildings built to house the livestock, which had been brought in the ship as frozen embryos and soon would be emerging from the incubators. And there the level land that in a few more months would be fields and gardens, and to the north the spaceship stood after years of roving. As he watched, the first bright star sprang out just beyond the spaceship's nose, and the spaceship and the star looked for all the world like a symbolic Christmas candle.

He walked down the hill, with the first night wind blowing in his face and the ancient smell of heather in the air, and was happy and exultant.

It was sinful, he thought, to be so joyful, but there was reason for it. The voyage had been happy and the planet-strike successful and here he was, the undisputed proprietor of an entire planet upon which, in the fullness of time, he would found a family and a dynasty. And he had all the time there was. There was no need to hurry. He had all of eternity if he needed it.

And, best of all, he had good companions.

They would be waiting for him when he stepped through the door. There would be laughter and a quick drink, then a leisurely dinner, and, later, brandy before the blazing fire. And there'd be talk—good talk, sober and intimate and friendly.

It had been the talk, he told himself, more than anything else, which had gotten them sanely through the century of space flight. That and their mutual love and appreciation of the finer points of the human culture—understanding of the arts, love of good literature, interest in philosophy. It was not often that six persons could live intimately for a hundred years without a single spat, without a touch of cabin fever.

Inside the manor house, they would be waiting for him in the fire- and candlelight, with the drinks all mixed and the talk already started, and the room would be warm with good fellowship and perfect understanding.

Cranford-Adams would be sitting in the big chair before the fire, staring at the flames and thinking, for he was the thinker of the group. And Allyn-Burbage would be standing, with one elbow on the mantel, a glass clutched in his hand and in his eyes the twinkle of good humor. Cosette-Middleton would be talking with him and laughing, for she was the gay one, with her elfin spirit and her golden hair. Anna-Quinze more than likely would be reading, curled up in a chair, and Mary-Foyle would be simply waiting, glad to be alive, glad to be with friends.

These, he thought, were the long companions of the trip, so full of understanding, so tolerant and gracious that a century had not dulled the beauty of their friendship.

Winston-Kirby hurried, a thing he almost never did, at the thought of those five who were waiting for him, anxious to be with them, to tell them of his walk across the moor, to discuss with them still again some details of their plans.

He turned into the walk. The wind was becoming cold, as it always did with the fall of darkness, and he raised the collar of his jacket for the poor protection it afforded.

He reached the door and stood for an instant in the chill, to savor the never-failing satisfaction of the massive timbering and the stout, strong squareness of the house. A place built to stand through the centuries, he thought, a place of dynasty with a sense of foreverness.

He pressed the latch and thrust his weight against the door and it came slowly open. A blast of warm air rushed out to greet him. He stepped into the entry hall and closed the door behind him. As he took off his cap and jacket and found a place to hang them, he stamped and scuffed his feet a little to let the others know that he had returned.

But there were no greetings for him, no sound of happy laughter. There was only silence from the inner room.

He turned about so swiftly that his hand trailed across his jacket and dislodged it from the hook. It fell to the floor with a smooth rustle of fabric and lay there, a little mound of cloth.

His legs suddenly were cold and heavy, and when he tried to hurry, the best he could do was shuffle, and he felt the chill edge of fear.

He reached the entrance to the room and stopped, shocked into immobility. His hands went out and grasped the door jamb on either side of him.

There was no one in the room. And not only that—the room itself was different. It was not simply the companions who were gone. Gone, as well, were the rich furnishings of the room, gone the comfort and the pride.

There were no rugs upon the floor, no hangings at the windows, no paintings on the wall. The fireplace was a naked thing of rough and jagged stone. The furniture—the little there was—was primitive, barely knocked together. A small trestle table stood before the fireplace, with a three-legged stool pulled up to a place that was set for one.

Winston-Kirby tried to call. The first time, the words gurgled in his throat and he could not get them out. He tried again and made it: "Job! Job, where are you?"

Job came running from somewhere in the house. "What's the trouble, sir?"

"Where are the others? Where have they gone? They should be waiting for me."

Job shook his head, just slightly, a quick move right and left: "Mister Kirby, sir, they were never here."

"Never here! But they were here when I left this morning. They knew I'd be coming back."

"You fail to understand, sir. There were never any others. There were just you and I and the other robots. And the embryos, of course."

Winston-Kirby let go of the door and walked a few feet forward.

"Job," he said, "you're joking." But he knew something was wrong—robots never joke.

"We let you keep them as long as we could," said Job. "We hated to have to take them from you, sir. But we needed the equipment for the incubators."

"But this room! The rugs, the furniture, the—"

"That was all part of it, sir. Part of the dimensino."

Winston-Kirby walked slowly across the room, used one foot to hook the three-legged stool out from the table. He sat down heavily.

"The dimensino?" he asked.

"Surely you remember."

He frowned to indicate he didn't. But it was coming back to him, some of it, slowly and reluctantly, emerging vaguely after all the years of forgetfulness.

He fought against the remembering and the knowledge. He tried to push it back into that dark corner of his mind from which it came. It was sacrilege and treason—it was madness.

"The human embryos," Job told him, "came through

88

very well. Of the thousand of them, all but three are visible."

Winston-Kirby shook his head, as if to clear away the mist that befogged his brain.

"We have the incubators all set up in the outbuildings, sir," said Job. "We waited as long as we could before we took the dimensino equipment. We let you have it until the very last. It might have been easier, sir, if we could have done it gradually, but there is no provision for that. You either have dimensino or you haven't got it."

"Of course," said Winston-Kirby, mumbling just a little. "It was considerate of you. I thank you very much."

He stood up unsteadily and rubbed his hand across his eyes.

"It's not possible," he said. "It simply can't *be* possible. I lived for a hundred years with them. They were as real as I am. They were flesh and blood, I tell you. They were . . ."

The room still was bare and empty, a mocking emptiness, an alien mockery.

"It is possible," said Job gently. "It is just the way it should be. Everything has gone according to the book. You are here, still sane, thanks to the dimensino. The embryos came through better than expected. The equipment is intact. In eight months or so, the children will be coming from the incubators. By that time, we will have gardens and a crop on the way. The livestock embryos will also have emerged and the colony will be largely self-sustaining."

Winston-Kirby strode to the table, picked up the plate that was laid at the single place. It was lightweight plastic.

"Tell me," he said. "Have we any china? Have we any glassware or silver?"

Job looked as near to startled as a robot ever could. "Of course not, sir. We had no room for more than just the bare essentials this trip. The china and the silver and all the rest of it will have to wait until much later."

"And I have been eating ship rations?"

"Naturally," said Job. "There was so little room and so much we had to take . . ."

Winston-Kirby stood with the plate in his hand, tapping it gently on the table, remembering those other dinners—aboard the ship and since the ship had landed—the steaming soup in its satiny tureen, the pink and juicy prime ribs, the huge potatoes baked to a mealy turn, the crisp green lettuce, the shine of polished silver, the soft sheen of good china, the—

"Job," he said.

"Sir?"

"It was all delusion, then?"

"I am afraid it was. I am sorry, sir."

"And you robots?"

"All of us are fine, sir. It was different with us. We can face reality."

"And humans can't."

"Sometimes it is better if they can be protected from it."

"But not now?"

"Not any more," said Job. "It must be faced now, sir."

Winston-Kirby laid the plate down on the table and turned back to the robot. "I think I'll go up to my room and change to other clothes. I presume dinner will be ready soon. Ship rations, doubtless?"

"A special treat tonight," Job told him. "Hezekiah found some lichens and I've made a pot of soup."

"Splendid!" Winston-Kirby said, trying not to gag.

He climbed the stairs to the door at the head of the stairs.

As he was about to go into the room, another robot came tramping down the hall.

"Good evening, sir," it said.

"And who are you?"

"I'm Solomon," said the robot. "I'm fixing up the nurseries."

"Soundproofing them, I hope."

"Oh, nothing like that. We haven't the material or time."

"Well, carry on," said Winston-Kirby, and went into the room.

It was not his room at all. It was small and plain. There was a bunk instead of the great four-poster he had been

90

sleeping in and there were no rugs, no full-length mirror, no easy chairs.

Delusion, he had said, not really believing it.

But here there was no delusion.

The room was cold with a dread reality—a reality, he knew, that had been long delayed. In the loneliness of this tiny room, he came face to face with it and felt the sick sense of loss. It was a reckoning that had been extended into the future as far as it might be—and extended not alone as a matter of mercy, of mere consideration, but because of a cold, hard necessity, a practical concession to human vulnerability.

For no man, no matter how well adjusted, no matter if immortal, could survive intact, in mind and body, a trip such as he had made. To survive a century under space conditions, there must be delusion and companionship to provide security and purpose from day to day. And that companionship must be more than human. For mere human companionship, however ideal, would give rise to countless irritations, would breed deadly cabin fever.

Dimensino companionship was the answer, then, providing an illusion of companionship flexible to every mood and need of the human subject. Providing, as well, a background to that companionship—a wish-fulfillment way of life that nailed down security such as humans under normal circumstances never could have known.

He sat down on the bunk and began to unlace his heavy walking shoes.

The practical human race, he thought—practical to the point of fooling itself to reach destination, practical to the point of fabricating the dimensino equipment to specifications which could be utilized, upon arrival, in the incubators.

But willing to gamble when there was a need to gamble. Ready to bet that a man could survive a century in space if he were sufficiently insulated against reality—insulated by seeming flesh and blood which, in sober fact, existed only by the courtesy of the human mind assisted by intricate electronics.

For no ship before had ever gone so far on a colonizing mission. No man had ever existed for even half as long under the influence of dimensino.

But there were few planets where Man might plant a colony under natural conditions, without extensive and expensive installations and precautions. The nearer of these planets had been colonized and the survey had shown that this one which he finally had reached was especially attractive.

So Earth and Man had bet. Especially one man, Winston-Kirby told himself with pride, but the pride was bitter in his mouth. The odds, he recalled, had been five to three against him.

And yet, even in his bitterness, he recognized the significance of what he had done. It was another breakthrough, another triumph for the busy little brain that was hammering at the door of all eternity.

It meant that the Galaxy was open, that Earth could remain the center of an expanding empire, that dimensino and immortal could travel to the very edge of space, that the seed of Man would be scattered wide and far, traveling as frozen embryos through the cold, black distance which hurt the mind to think of.

He went to the small chest of drawers and found a change of clothing, laid it on the bunk and began to take off his hiking outfit.

Everything was going according to the book, Job had said.

The house was bigger than he had wanted it, but the robots had been right—a big building would be needed to house a thousand babies. The incubators were set up and the nurseries were being readied and another far Earth colony was getting under way.

And colonies were important, he remembered, reaching back into that day, a hundred years before, when he and many others had laid their plans—including the plan

92

whereby he could delude himself and thus preserve his sanity. For with more and more of the immortal mutations occurring, the day was not too distant when the human race would require all the room that it could grab.

And it was the mutant immortals who were the key persons in the colonizing programs—going out as founding fathers to supervise the beginning of each colony, staying on as long as needed, to act as a sort of elder statesman until that day when the colony could stand on its own feet.

There would be busy years ahead, he knew, serving as father, proctor, judge, sage and administrator, a sort of glorified Old Man of a brand-new tribe.

He pulled on his trousers, scuffed his feet into his shoes, rose to tuck in his shirt tail. And he turned, by force of habit, to the full-length mirror.

And the glass was there!

He stood astounded, gaping foolishly at the image of himself. And behind him, in the glass, he saw the great four-poster and the easy chairs.

He swung around and the bed and chairs were gone. There were just the bunk and the chest of drawers in the small, mean room.

Slowly he sat down on the edge of the bunk, clasping his hands so they wouldn't shake.

It wasn't true! It couldn't be! The dimensino was gone.

And yet it was with him still, lurking in his brain, just around the corner if he would only try.

He tried and it was easy. The room changed as he remembered it—with the full-length mirror and the massive bed upon which he sat, the thick rugs, the gleaming liquor cabinet and the tasteful drapes.

He tried to make it go away, barely remembering back in some deep, black closet of his mind that he must make it go.

But it wouldn't go away.

He tried and tried again, and it still was there, and he felt the will to make it go, slipping from his consciousness.

"No!" he cried in terror, and the terror did it.

He sat in the small, bare room.

He found that he was breathing hard, as if he'd climbed a high, steep hill. His hands were fists and his teeth were clenched and he felt the sweat trickling down his ribs.

It would be easy, he thought, so easy and so pleasant to slip back to the old security, to the warm, deep friendship, to the lack of pressing purpose.

But he must not do it, for here was a job to do. Distasteful as it seemed now, as cold, as barren, it still was something he must do. For it was more than just one more colony. It was the breakthrough, the sure and certain knowledge, the proved knowledge, that Man no longer was chained by time or distance.

And yet there was this danger to be recognized; it was not something on which one might shut one's mind. It must be reported in every clinical detail so that, back on Earth, it must be studied and the inherent menace somehow remedied or removed.

Side effect, he wondered, or simply a matter of learning? For the dimensino was no more than an aid to the human mind—an aid to a very curious end, the production of controlled hallucinations operating on the wish-fulfillment level.

After a hundred years, perhaps, the human mind had learned the technique well, so well that there was no longer need of the dimensino.

It was something he should have realized, he insisted to himself. He had gone on long walks and, during all those hours alone, the delusion had not faded. It had taken the sudden shock of silence and emptiness, where he had expected laughter and warm greeting, to penetrate the haze of delusion in which he'd walked for years. And even now it lurked, a conditioned state of mind, to ambush him at every hidden thicket.

How long would it be before the ability would start to wear away? What might be done to wipe it out entirely? How does one unlearn a thing he's spent a century in learning? Exactly how dangerous was it—was there neces-

94

sity of a conscious thought, an absolute command or could a man slip into it simply as an involuntary retreat from drear reality?

He must warn the robots. He must talk it over with them. Some sort of emergency measure must be set up to protect him against the wish or urge, some manner of drastic action be devised to rescue him, should he slip back into the old delusion.

Although, he thought, it would be so fine to walk out of the room and down the stairs and find the others waiting for him, with the drinks all ready and the talk well started. . . .

"Cut it out!" he screamed.

Wipe it from his mind—that was what he must do. He must not even think of it. He must work so hard that he would have no time to think, become so tired from work that he'd fall into bed and go to sleep at once and have no chance to dream.

He ran through his mind all that must be done—the watching of the incubators, preparing the ground for gardens and for crops, servicing the atomic generators, getting in timbers against the need of building, exploring and mapping and surveying the adjacent territory, overhauling the ship for the one-robot return flight to Earth.

He filled his mind with it. He tagged items for further thought and action. He planned the days and months and years ahead. And at last he was satisfied.

He had it under control.

He tied his shoes and finished buttoning his shirt. Then, with a resolute tread, he opened the door and walked out on the landing.

A hum of talk floating up the stairway stopped him in his tracks.

Fear washed over him. Then the fear evaporated. Gladness burst within him and he took a quick step forward.

At the top of the stairs, he halted and reached out a hand to grasp the banister.

Alarm bells were ringing in his brain and the gladness

fell away. There was nothing left but sorrow, a terrible, awful grieving.

He could see one corner of the room below and he could see that it was carpeted. He could see the drapes and paintings and one ornate golden chair.

With a moan, he turned and fled to his room. He slammed the door and stood with his back against it.

The room was the way it should be, bare and plain and cold.

Thank God, he thought. Thank God!

A shout came up the stairway.

"Winston, what's wrong with you? Winston, hurry up!"

And another voice: "Winston, we're celebrating. We have a suckling pig."

And still another voice: "With an apple in its mouth."

He didn't answer.

They'll go away, he thought. They have to go away.

And even as he thought it, half of him—more than half— longed in sudden agony to open up the door and go down the stairs and know once again the old security and the ancient friendship.

He found that he had both his hands behind his back and that they were clutching the doorknob as if they were frozen there.

He heard steps on the stairway, the sound of many happy, friendly voices, coming up to get him.

Idiot's Crusade

FOR A LONG TIME I was the village idiot, but not any longer
—although they call me "dummy" still and even worse than
that.

I'm a genius now, but I won't let them know.

Not ever.

If they found out, they'd be on their guard against me.

No one has suspected me and no one will. My shuffle is
the same and my gaze as vacant and my mumblings just
as vague as they ever were. At times, it has been hard to
remember to keep the shuffle and the gaze and mumblings
as they were before, times when it was hard not to overdo
them. But it's important not to arouse suspicion.

It all started the morning I went fishing.

I told Ma I was going fishing while we were eating
breakfast and she didn't object. She knows I like fishing.
When I fish, I don't get into trouble.

"All right, Jim," she said. "Some fish will taste real
good."

"I know where to get them," I told her. "That hole in the
creek just past Alf Adams' place."

"Now don't you get into any fracas with Alf," Ma
warned me. "Just because you don't like him—"

"He was mean to me. He worked me harder than he
should have. And he cheated me out of my pay. And he
laughs at me."

I shouldn't have said that, because it hurts Ma when I
say someone laughs at me.

"You mustn't pay attention to what people do," said Ma,

speaking kind and gentle. "Remember what Preacher Martin said last Sunday. He said—"

"I know what he said, but I still don't like being laughed at. People shouldn't laugh at me."

"No," Ma agreed, looking sad. "They shouldn't."

I went on eating my breakfast, thinking that Preacher Martin was a great one to be talking about humility and patience, knowing the kind of man he was and how he was carrying on with Jennie Smith, the organist. He was a great one to talk about anything at all.

After breakfast, I went out to the woodshed to get my fishing tackle and Bounce came across the street to help me. After Ma, Bounce is the best friend I have. He can't talk to me, of course—not actually, that is—but neither does he laugh at me.

I talked to him while I was digging worms and asked him if he wanted to go fishing with me. I could see he did, so I went across the street to tell Mrs. Lawson that Bounce was going along. He belonged to her, but he spent most of his time with me.

We started out, me carrying my cane pole and all my fishing stuff and Bounce walking at my heels, as if I were someone he was proud to be seen walking with.

We went past the bank, where Banker Patton was sitting in the big front window, working at his desk and looking like the most important man in all of Mapleton, which he was. I went by slow so I could hate him good.

Ma and me wouldn't be living in the old tumbledown house we're living in if Banker Patton hadn't foreclosed on our home after Pa died.

We went out past Alf Adams' place, which is the first farm out of town, and I hated him some, too, but not as hard as Banker Patton. All Alf had done was work me harder than he should have, then cheat me out of my pay.

Alf was a big, blustery man and a good enough farmer, I guess—at least he made it pay. He had a big new barn and it's just like him not to paint it red, the way any proper barn is painted, but white with red trim. Who ever heard of paint trim on a barn?

Just beyond Alf's place, Bounce and I turned off the road and went down across the pasture, heading for the big hole in the creek.

Alf's prize Hereford bull was way off in another corner of the pasture with the rest of the stock. When he saw us, he started coming for us, not mean or belligerent, but just investigating and ready for a fight if one was offered him. I wasn't afraid of him, because I'd made friends with him that summer I had worked for Alf. I used to pet him and scratch behind his ears. Alf said I was a crazy fool and someday the bull would kill me.

"You can never trust a bull," Alf said.

When the bull was near enough to see who it was, he knew we meant no harm, so he went back across the pasture again.

We got to the hole and I started fishing, while Bounce went up the stream to do some investigating. I caught a few fish, but they weren't very big and they weren't biting very often and I got disinterested. I like to fish, but to keep my interest up, I have to catch some.

So I got to daydreaming. I began wondering if you marked off a certain area of ground—a hundred feet square, say—and went over it real careful, how many different kinds of plants you'd find. I looked over a patch of ground next to where I was sitting and I could see just ordinary pasture grass and some dandelions and some dock and a couple of violets, and a buttercup which didn't have any flowers as yet.

Suddenly, when I was looking at the dandelion, I realized I could see *all* that dandelion, not just the part that showed above the ground!

I don't know how long I'd been seeing it that way before realizing it. And I'm not certain that "seeing" is the right word. Maybe "know" would be better. I *knew* how that dandelion's big taproot went down into the ground and how the little feathery roots grew out of it, and I knew where all the roots were, how they were taking water and chemicals out of the ground, how reserve food was stored in the root and how the dandelion used the sunlight to convert its food into a form it could use. And the funniest thing about it was that I had never known any of it before.

I looked at the other plants and I could see all of them the same way. I wondered if something had gone wrong with my eyes and if I would have to go around looking into things instead of at them, so I tried to make the new seeing go away and it did.

Then I tried to see the dandelion root again and I saw it, just the way I had before.

I sat there, wondering why I had never been able to see that way before and why I was able to now. And while I was wondering, I looked into the pool and tried to see down into the pool and I could, just as plain as day. I could see clear to the bottom of it and into all the corners of it, and there were lunkers lying in there, bigger than any fish that ever had been taken from the creek.

I saw that my bait was nowhere near any of the fish, so I moved it over until it was just in front of the nose of one of the biggest ones. But the fish didn't seem to see it, or if he did, he wasn't hungry, for he just lay there, fanning the water with his fins and making his gills work.

I moved the bait down until it bumped his nose, but he still didn't pay any attention to it.

So I made the fish hungry.

Don't ask me how I did it. I can't tell you. I all at once knew I could and just how to do it. So I made him hungry and he went for that bait like Bounce grabbing a bone.

He pulled the cork clear under and I heaved on the pole and hoisted him out. I took him off the hook and put him on the stringer, along with the four or five little ones I'd caught.

Then I picked out another big fish and lowered my bait down to him and made him hungry.

In the next hour and a half, I just about cleaned out all

the big fish. There were some little ones left, but I didn't bother with them. I had the stringer almost full and I couldn't carry it in my hand, for then the fish would have dragged along the ground. I had to sling it over my shoulder and those fish felt awfully wet.

I called Bounce and went back to town.

Everyone I met stopped and had a look at my fish and wanted to know where I'd got them and what I'd caught them on and if there were any left or had I taken them all. When I told them I'd taken all there was, they laughed fit to kill.

I was just turning off Main Street on my way home when Banker Patton stepped out of the barber shop. He smelled nice from the bottles of stuff that Jake, the barber, uses on his customers.

He saw me with my fish and stopped in front of me. He looked at me and looked at the fish and he rubbed his fat hands together. Then he said, like he was talking to a child, "Why, Jimmy, where did you get all those fish?" He sounded a little bit, too, like I might not have a right to them and probably had used some lowdown trick to get them.

"Out in the hole on Alf's place," I told him.

All at once, without even trying to do it, I saw him the same way I had seen the dandelion—his stomach and intestines and something that must have been his liver—and up above them all, surrounded by a doughy mass of pink, a pulsating thing that I knew must be his heart.

I guess that's the first time anybody ever *really* hated someone else's guts.

I shot out my hands—well, not my hands, for one was clutching the cane pole and the other was busy with the fish—but it felt almost exactly as if I'd put them out and grabbed his heart and squeezed it hard.

He gasped once, then sighed and wilted, like all the starch had gone out of him, and I had to jump out of the way so he wouldn't bump into me when he fell.

He never moved after he hit the ground.

101

Jake came running out of his barber shop.

"What happened to him?" he asked me.

"He just fell over," I said.

Jake looked at him. "It's a heart attack. I'd know it anywhere. I'll run for Doc."

He took off up the street for Doc Mason while other people came hurrying out of the places along the street.

There was Ben from the cheese factory and Mike from the pool hall and a couple of farmers who were in the general store.

I got out of there and went on home and Ma was pleased with the fish.

"They'll taste real good," she said, looking at them. "How did you come to catch that many, Jim?"

"They were biting good," I said.

"Well, you hurry up and clean them. We'll have to eat some right away and I'll take some over to Preacher Martin's and I'll rub salt in the others and put them in the cellar where it's good and cool. They'll keep for several days."

Just then, Mrs. Lawson ran across the street and told Ma about Banker Patton.

"He was talking to Jim when it happened," she told Ma.

Ma said to me, "Why didn't you tell me, Jim?"

"I never got around to it," I said. "I was showing you these fish."

So the two of them went on talking about Banker Patton and I went out to the woodshed and cleaned the fish. Bounce sat alongside me and watched me do it and I swear he was as happy over those fish as I was, just like he might have had a hand in catching them.

"It was a nice day, Bounce," I said and Bounce said he'd thought so, too. He recalled running up and down the stream and how he'd chased a frog and the good smell there was when he stuck his nose down to the ground and sniffed.

Now I don't want you to think I'm trying to make you

believe Bounce actually talked, because he didn't. But it was just as if he'd said those very words.

People all the time are laughing at me and making cracks about me and trying to bait me because I'm the village idiot, but there are times when the village idiot has it over all of them. They would have been scared they were going crazy if a dog talked to them, but I didn't think it was strange at all. I just thought how much nicer it was now that Bounce could talk and how I wouldn't have to guess at what he wanted to say. I never thought it was queer at all, because I always figured Bounce could talk if he only tried, being a smart dog.

So Bounce and I sat there and talked while I cleaned the fish. When I came out of the woodshed, Mrs. Lawson had gone home and Ma was in the kitchen, getting a skillet ready to cook some of the fish.

"Jim, you . . ." she hesitated, then went on, "Jim, you didn't have anything to do with what happened to Banker Patton, did you? You didn't push him or hit him or anything?"

"I never even touched him," I said and that was true. I certainly hadn't touched him.

In the afternoon, I went out and worked in the garden. Ma does some housework now and then and that brings in some money, but we couldn't get along if it wasn't for the garden. I used to work some, but since the fight I had with Alf over him not paying me, she don't let me work for anyone. She says if I take care of the garden and catch some fish, I'm helping out enough.

Working in the garden, I found a different use for my new way of seeing. There were worms in the cabbages and I could see every one of them and I killed them all by squeezing them, the way I'd squeezed Banker Patton. I found a cloudy sort of stuff on some of the tomato plants and I suppose it was some kind of virus, because it was so small I could hardly see it at first. So I magnified it and could see it fine, and I made it go way. I didn't squeeze it like I did the worms. I just made it go away.

It was fun working in the garden, when you could look down into the ground and see how the parsnips and radishes were coming and could kill the cutworms you found there, and know just how the soil was and if everything was all right.

We'd had fish for lunch and we had fish again for supper, and after supper I went for a walk.

Before I knew it, I was walking by Banker Patton's place and, going past, I felt the grief inside the house.

I stood out on the sidewalk and let the grief come into me. I suppose that outside any house in town, I could have felt just as easily whatever was going on inside, but I hadn't known I could and I hadn't tried. It was only because the grief in the Patton house was so deep and strong that I noticed it.

The banker's oldest daughter was upstairs in her room and I could feel her crying. The other daughter was sitting with her mother in the living room and neither of them was crying, but they seemed lost and lonely. There were other people in the house, but they weren't very sad. Some neighbors, probably, who'd come in to keep the family company.

I felt sorry for the three of them and I wanted to help them. Not that I'd done anything wrong in killing Banker Patton, but I felt sorry for those women, because, after all, it wasn't their fault the way Banker Patton was, so I stood there, wishing I could help them.

And all at once I felt that perhaps I could and I tried first with the daughter who was upstairs in her room. I reached out to her and I told her happy thoughts. It wasn't easy to start with, but pretty soon I got the hang of it and it wasn't hard to make her happy. Then I made the other two happy and went on my way, feeling better about what I'd done to the family.

I listened in on the houses I passed. Most of them were happy, or at least contented, though I found a couple that were sad. Automatically, I reached out my mind and gave them happiness. It wasn't that I felt I should do something

104

good for any particular person. To tell the truth, I don't remember which houses I made happy. I just thought if I was able to do a thing like that, I should do it. It wasn't right for someone to have that kind of power and refuse to use it.

Ma was sitting up for me when I got home. She was looking kind of worried, the way she always does when I disappear for a long time and she don't know where I am.

I went up to my room and got into bed and lay awake for a long time, wondering how come I could do all the things I could and how, suddenly, today I was able to do them when I'd never been able to before. But finally I went to sleep.

The situation is not ideal, of course, but a good deal better than I had any reason to expect. It is not likely that one should find on every alien planet a host so made to order for our purpose as is this one of mine.

It has accepted me without recognizing me, has made no attempt to deny itself to me or to reject me. It is of an order of intelligence which has enabled it, quickly and efficiently, to make use of those most-readily manipulated of my abilities and this has aided me greatly in my observations. It is fairly mobile and consorts freely with its kind, which are other distinct advantages.

I reckon myself fortunate, indeed, to have found so satisfactory a host so soon upon arrival.

When I got up and had breakfast, I went outside and found Bounce waiting for me. He said he wanted to go and chase some rabbits and I agreed to go along. He said since we could talk now, we ought to make a good team. I could stand up on a stump or a pile of rocks or even climb a tree, so I could overlook the ground and see the rabbit and yell out to him which way it was going, and he could intercept it.

We went up the road toward Alf's place, but turned off

down across the pasture, heading for some cut-over land on the hill across the creek.

When we were off the road, I turned around to give Alf a good hating and while I was standing there, hating him, a thought came into my mind, I didn't know if I could do it, but it seemed to be a good idea, so I tried.

I moved my seeing up to Alf's barn and went right through and came out in the middle of the haymow, with hay packed all around me. But all the time, you understand, I was standing out there in the pasture with Bounce, on our way to chase some rabbits.

I'd like to explain what I did next and how I did it, but mostly what worries me is how I knew enough to do it— I mean enough about chemical reaction and stuff like that. I did something to the hay and something to the oxygen and I started a fire up there in the center of the haymow. When I saw it was started good, I got out of there and was in myself again and Bounce and I went across the creek and up the hill.

I kept looking back over my shoulder, wondering if the fire might not have gone out, but all at once there was a little trickle of smoke coming out of the haymow opening up under the gable's end.

We'd got up into the cut-over land by that time and I sat down on a stump and enjoyed myself. The fire had a good start before it busted out and there wasn't a thing that could be done to save the barn. It went up with a roar and made the prettiest column of smoke you've ever seen.

On the way home, I stopped at the general store. Alf was there and he seemed much too happy to have just lost his barn.

But it wasn't long until I understood why he was so happy.

"I had her insured," he told Bert Jones, the storekeeper, "plumb up to the hilt. Anyhow, it was too big a barn, a lot bigger than I needed. When I built it, I figured I was

106

going to go into milking heavier than I've done and would need the space."

Bert chuckled. "Handy fire for you, Alf."

"Best thing that ever happened to me. I can build another barn and have some cash left over."

I was pretty sore about bungling it, but I thought of a way to get even.

After lunch, I went up the road again and out into Alf's pasture and hunted up the bull. He was glad to see me, although he did a little pawing and some bellowing just to show off.

I had wondered all the way out if I could talk to the bull the way I talked to Bounce and I was afraid that maybe I couldn't, for Bounce was bound to be smarter than a bull.

I was right, of course. It was awful hard to make that bull understand anything.

I made the mistake of scratching behind his ears while I tried to talk to him and he almost went to sleep. I could feel just how good the scratching felt to him. So I hauled off and kicked him in the ribs to wake him up, so he would pay attention. He did pay a little closer attention and even did a little answering, but not much. A bull is awful dumb.

But I felt fairly sure I'd got my idea across, for he started acting sore and feisty and I'm afraid that I overdid it just a mite. I made it to the fence ahead of him and went over without even touching it. The bull stopped at the fence and stood there, pawing and raising Cain, and I got out of there as fast as I could go.

I went home fairly pleased with myself for thinking up as smart a thing as that. I wasn't surprised in the least to hear that evening that Alf had been killed by his bull.

It wasn't a pretty way to die, of course, but Alf had it coming to him, the way he beat me out of my summer wages.

I was sitting in the pool hall when the news was brought in by someone and they all talked about it. Some said Alf had always claimed you couldn't trust no bull, and some-one else said he'd often said I was the only one who'd ever gotten along with this particular bull and he was scared all the time I was there for fear the bull would kill me.

They saw me sitting there and they asked me about it and I acted dumb and all of them laughed at me, but I didn't mind their laughing. I knew something they didn't know. Imagine how surprised they'd be if they ever learned the truth!

They won't, of course.

I'm too smart for that.

When I went home, I got a tablet and a pencil and started to write down the names of all my enemies—every-one who had ever laughed at me or done mean things to me or said mean things about me.

The list was pretty long. It included almost everyone in town.

I sat there thinking and I decided maybe I shouldn't kill everyone in town. Not that I couldn't, for I could have, just as slick as anything. But thinking about Alf and Banker Patton, I could see there wasn't any lasting satis-faction in killing people you hate. And I could see as plain as day that if you killed a lot of people, it could leave you pretty lonesome.

I read down through the list of names I'd made and I gave a couple of them the benefit of a doubt and scratched them out. I read those that were left over and I had to admit that every one of them was bad. I decided that if I didn't kill them, I'd have to do something else about them, for I couldn't let them go on being bad.

I thought about it a long time and I remembered some of the things I'd heard Preacher Martin say, although, as I've mentioned before, he's a great one to be saying them. I decided I'd have to lay aside my hate and return good for evil.

I am puzzled and disturbed, although that, perhaps, is the normal reaction when one attaches oneself to an alien being. This is a treacherous and unprincipled species and, as such, an incalculably important one to study.

I am continually amazed at the facility with which my host has acquired the use of my talents, continually appalled by the use he makes of them. I am more than puzzled by his own conviction that he is less intelligent than his fellows; his actions during my acquaintance with him do not bear this out. I wonder if it may not be a racial trait, a sort of cult-attitude of inferiority, that it may be ill-mannered to think of oneself in any other way.

But I half suspect that he may have sensed me in some way without my knowing it and may be employing this strange concept as a device to force me from his mind. Under such a circumstance, it would not be prime ethics for me to remain with him—but he has proved to be such an excellent seat of observation that I am loath to leave him.

The fact is, I don't know. I could, of course, seize control of his mind and thus learn the truth of this and other matters which are perplexing me. But I fear that, in doing so, I would destroy his effectiveness as a free agent and thus impair his observational value. I have decided to wait before using such a drastic measure.

I ate breakfast in a hurry, being anxious to get started. Ma asked me what I was going to do and I said just walk around a bit.

First off, I went to the parsonage and sat down outside the hedge between it and the church. Pretty soon, Preacher Martin came out and began to walk up and down in what he called his garden, pretending he was sunk in holy thought, although I always suspected it was just an act to impress old ladies who might see him.

I put out my mind real easy and finally I got it locked with his so neatly, it seemed that it was me, not him, who was walking up and down. It was a queer feeling, I can tell you, for all the time I knew good and well that I was sitting there back of the hedge.

He wasn't thinking any holy thoughts at all. He was going over in his mind all the arguments he intended to use to hit up the church board for a raise in salary. He was doing some minor cussing out of some of the members of the board for being tight-fisted skinflints and that I agreed with, because they surely were.

Taking it easy, just sort of stealing in on his thought, I made him think about Jennie Smith, the organist, and the way he was carrying on with her, and I made him ashamed of himself for doing it.

He tried to push me away, though he didn't know it was me; he just thought it was his own mind bringing up the matter. But I wouldn't let him push the thought away. I piled it on real heavy.

I made him think how the people in the church trusted him and looked to him for spiritual leadership, and I made him remember back to when he was a younger man, just out of seminary, and looked on his lifetime work as a great crusade. I made him think of how he'd betrayed all the things he'd believed in then, and I got him down so low, he was almost bawling. Then I made him tell himself that owning up was the only way he could absolve himself. Once he'd done that, he could start life over again and be a credit to himself and his church.

I went away, figuring I'd done a fair job of work on him, but knowing that I'd have to check up on him every now and then.

At the general store, I sat around and watched Bert Jones sweep out the place. While he was talking to me, I sneaked into his mind and recalled to him all the times he'd paid way less than market prices for the eggs the farmers brought in, and the habit of sneaking in extra items on the bills he sent out to his charge customers, and how he'd cheated on his income tax. I scared him plenty on the income tax and I kept working at him until he'd about decided to make it right with everyone he'd cheated.

I didn't finish the job airtight, but I knew I could come back any time I wanted to and, in a little while, I'd make an honest man of Bert.

Over at the barber shop, I watched Jake cut a head of hair. I wasn't too interested in the man Jake was working on—he lived four or five miles out of town—and at the moment, I figured that I'd better confine my work to the people in the village.

Before I left, I had Jake plenty worried about the gambling he'd been doing in the back room at the pool hall and had him almost ready to make a clean breast of it to his wife.

I went over to the pool hall. Mike was sitting back of the counter with his hat on, reading the baseball scores in the morning paper. I got a day-old paper and pretended to read it. Mike laughed and asked me when I'd learned to read, so I laid it on good and thick.

When I left, I knew, just as soon as I was out the door, he'd go down into the basement and dump all the moonshine down the drain, and before too long, I'd get him to close up the back room.

Over at the cheese factory, I didn't have much chance to work on Ben. The farmers were bringing in their milk and he was too busy for me to really get into his mind. But I did manage to make him think of what would happen if Jake ever caught him with Jake's wife. And I knew when I could catch him alone, I could do a top-notch job on him, for I saw he scared easy.

And that's the way it went.

It was tough work and at times I felt it was just too much of a job. But then I'd sit down and remind myself that it was my duty to keep on—that for some reason this power had been given me and that it was up to me to use it for all it was worth. And furthermore, I was not to use it for myself, for any selfish ends, but for the good of other people.

I don't think I missed a person in the village.

Remember how we wondered if there might not be un-seen flaws in this plan of ours? We went over it most carefully and could find none, yet all of us feared that some might show up in actual practice. Now I can report there is one. It is this:

Accurate, impersonal observation is impossible, for as soon as one introduces one's self into a host, his abilities become available to the host and at once become a factor which upsets the norm.

As a result of this, I am getting a distorted picture of the culture of this planet. Reluctant to intervene before, I am now convinced that I must move to take command of the situation.

Bert, now that he's turned honest, is the happiest man you ever saw. Even losing all the customers who got sore at him when he explained why he paid them back some money doesn't bother him. I don't know how Ben is get-ting along—he disappeared right after Jake took the shot-gun to him. But, then, everyone agrees Ben was overdoing it when he went to Jake and told him he was sorry for what had been going on. Jake's wife is gone, too, and some folks say she followed Ben.

To tell the truth, I am well satisfied with the way every-thing's turned out. Everyone is honest and no one is fool-ing around with anyone else and there ain't a lick of gam-bling or drinking going on in town. Mapleton probably is the most moral village in the United States.

I feel that perhaps it turned out the way it did because I started out by conquering my own evil thoughts and, instead of killing all the folks I hated, set out to do them good.

I'm a little puzzled when I walk through the streets at night because I don't pick up near as many happy thoughts as I used to. In fact, there are times when it keeps me busy almost all night long, getting them cheered up. You'd think honest folks would be happy folks. I imagine it's because, now they're good instead of bad, they're not so given to giddy pleasures, but are more concerned with the solid, worth-while side of life.

I'm a little worried about myself. While I did a lot of good, I may have done it for a selfish reason. I did it, perhaps partly, to make up for killing Alf and Banker Patton. And I did it not for just people, but for people I know. That doesn't seem right. Why should only people I know benefit?

Help! Can you hear me? I'm trapped! I can neither control my host nor can I escape from him. Do not under any circumstances let anyone else try to use another member of this race as a host!
Help!
Can you hear me?
Help!

I've sat up all night, thinking, and now the way is clear.

Having reached my decision, I feel important and humble, both at once. I know I'm a chosen instrument for good and must not let anything stop me. I know the village was no more than a proving ground, a place for me to learn what I could really do. Knowing now, I'm determined to use the power to its utmost for the good of all humanity.

Ma's been saving up a little money for a long time for a decent burial.

I know just where she hides it.

It's all she's got.

But it's enough to get me to the U.N.

Death Scene

SHE WAS WAITING on the stoop of the house when he turned into the driveway and as he wheeled the car up the concrete and brought it to a halt he was certain she knew, too.

She had just come from the garden and had one arm full of flowers and she was smiling at him just a shade too gravely.

He carefully locked the car and put the keys away in the pocket of his jacket and reminded himself once again, "Matter-of-factly, friend. For it is better this way."

And that was the truth, he reassured himself. It was much better than the old way. It gave a man some time.

He was not the first and he would not be the last and for some of them it was rough, and for others, who had prepared themselves, it was not so rough and in time, perhaps, it would become a ritual so beautiful and so full of dignity one would look forward to it. It was more civilized and more dignified than the old way had been and in another hundred years or so there could be no doubt that it would become quite acceptable. All that was wrong with it now, he told himself, was that it was too new. It took a little time to become accustomed to this way of doing things after having done them differently through all of human history.

He got out of the car and went up the walk to where she waited for him. He stooped and kissed her and the kiss was a little longer than was their regular custom—and a bit more tender. And as he kissed her he smelled the summer flowers she carried, and he thought how appropriate it was that he should at this time smell the flowers from the garden they both loved.

"You know," he said and she nodded at him.

"Just a while ago," she said. "I knew you would be coming home. I went out and picked the flowers."

"The children will be coming, I imagine."

"Of course," she said. "They will come right away."

He looked at his watch, more from force of habit than a need to know the time. "There is time," he said. "Plenty of time for all of them to get here. I hope they bring the kids."

"Certainly they will," she said. "I went to phone them once, then I thought how silly."

He nodded. "We're of the old school, Florence. It's hard even yet to accept this thing—to know the children will know and come almost as soon as we know. It's still a little hard to be sure of a thing like that."

She patted his arm. "The family will be all together. There'll be time to talk. We'll have a splendid visit."

"Yes, of course," he said.

He opened the door for her and she stepped inside.

"What pretty flowers," he said.

"They've been the prettiest this year that they have ever been."

"That vase," he said. "The one you got last birthday. The blue and gold. That's the one to use."

"That's exactly what I thought. On the dining table."

She went to get the vase and he stood in the living room and thought how much he was a part of this room and this room a part of him. He knew every inch of it and it knew him as well and it was a friendly place, for he'd spent years making friends with it.

Here he'd walked the children of nights when they had been babies and been ill of cutting teeth or croup or colic, nights when the lights in this room had been the only lights in the entire block. Here the family had spent many evening hours in happiness and peace—and it had been a lovely thing, the peace. For he could remember the time when there had been no peace, nowhere in the world, and no thought or hope of peace, but in its place the ever-present dread and threat of war, a dread that had been so commonplace that you scarcely noticed it, a dread you came to think was a normal part of living.

Then, suddenly, there had been the dread no longer, for you could not fight a war if your enemy could look ahead an entire day and see what was about to happen. You could not fight a war and you could not play a game of baseball or any sort of game, you could not rob or cheat or murder, you could not make a killing in the market. There were a lot of things you could no longer do and there were times when it spoiled a lot of fun, for surprise and anticipation had been made impossible. It took a lot of getting used to and a lot of readjustment, but you were safe, at least, for there could be no war—not only at the moment, but forever and forever, and you knew that not only were you safe, but your children safe as well and their children and your children's children's children and you were willing to pay almost any sort of price for such complete assurance.

It is better this way, he told himself, standing in the friendly room. It is much better this way. Although at times it's hard.

He walked across the room and through it to the porch and stood on the porch steps looking at the flowers. Florence was right, he thought; they were prettier this year than any year before. He tried to remember back to some year when they might have been prettier, but he couldn't quite be sure. Maybe the autumn when young John had been a baby, for that year the mums and asters had been particularly fine. But that was unfair, he told himself, for it was not autumn now, but summer. It was impossible to compare summer flowers with autumn. Or the year when Mary had been ill so long—the lilacs had been so deeply purple and had smelled so sweet; he remembered bringing in great bouquets of them each evening because she loved them so. But that was no comparison, for the lilacs bloomed in spring.

A neighbor went past on the sidewalk outside the picket fence and he spoke gravely to her: "Good afternoon, Mrs. Abrams."

"Good afternoon, Mr. Williams," she said and that was the way it always was, except on occasions she would stop a moment and they'd talk about the flowers. But today she would not stop unless he made it plain he would like to have her stop, for otherwise she would not wish to intrude upon him.

That was the way it had been at the office, he recalled. He'd put away his work with sure and steady hands— as sure and steady as he could manage them. He'd walked to the rack and got down his hat and no one had spoken to him, not a single one of them had kidded him about his quitting early, for all had guessed—or known—as well as he. You could not always tell, of course, for the foresight ability was more pronounced in some than it was in others, although the lag in even the least efficient of them would not be more than a quarter-hour at most.

He'd often wished he could understand how it had been brought about, but there were factors involved he could not even remotely grasp. He knew the story, of course, for he could remember the night that it had happened and the excitement there had been—and the consternation. But knowing how it came about and the reason for it was quite a different thing from understanding it.

It had been an ace in the hole, a move of desperation to be used only as a last resort. The nation had been ready for a long time with the transmitters all set up and no one asking any questions because everyone had taken it for granted they were a part of the radar network and, in that case, the less said of them the better.

No one had wanted to use those transmitters, or at least that had been the official explanation after they'd been used—but anything was better than another war.

So the time had come, the time of last resort, the day

117

of desperation, and the switches had been flicked, blanketing the nation with radiations that did something to the brain—"stimulating latent abilities" was as close a general explanation as anyone had made—and all at once everyone had been able to see twenty-four hours ahead.

There'd been hell to pay, of course, for quite a little while, but after a time it simmered down and the people settled down to make the best of it, to adapt and live with their strange new ability.

The President had gone on television to tell the world what had happened and he had warned potential enemies that we'd know twenty-four hours ahead of time exactly what they'd do. In consequence of which they did exactly nothing except to undo a number of incriminating moves they had already made—some of which the President had foretold that they would undo, naming the hour and place and the manner of their action.

He had said the process was no secret and that other nations were welcome to the know-how if they wanted it, although it made but little difference if they did or not, for the radiations in time would spread throughout the entire world and would affect all people. It was a permanent change, he said, for the ability was inheritable and would be passed on from one generation to the next, and never again, for good or evil, would the human race be blind as it had been in the past.

So finally there had been peace, but there'd been a price to pay. Although, perhaps, not too great a price, Williams told himself. He'd liked baseball, he recalled, and there could be no baseball now, for it was a pointless thing to play a game the outcome of which you'd know a day ahead of time. He had liked to have the boys in occasionally for a round of poker—but poker was just as pointless now and as impossible as baseball or football or horse racing or any other sport.

There had been many changes, some of them quite awkward. Take newspapers, for example, and radio and television reporting of the news. Political tactics had been forced to undergo a change, somewhat for the better, and gambling and crime had largely disappeared.

Mostly, it had been for the best. Although even some of the best was a little hard at first—and some of it would take a long time to become completely accustomed to.

Take his own situation now, he thought.

A lot more civilized than in the old days, but still fairly hard to take. Hard especially on Florence and the children, forcing them into a new and strange attitude that in time would harden into custom and tradition, but now was merely something new and strange. But Florence was standing up to it admirably, he thought. They'd often talked of it, especially in these last few years, and they had agreed that no matter which of them it was they would keep it calm and dignified, for that was the only way to face it. It was one of the payments that you made for peace, although sometimes it was a little hard to look at it that way.

But there were certain compensations. Florence and he could have a long talk before the children arrived. There'd be a chance to go over certain final details—finances and insurance and other matters of like nature. Under the old way there would have been, he told himself, no chance at all for that. There'd be the opportunity to do all the little worthwhile things, all the final sentimental gestures, that except for the foresight ability would have been denied.

There'd be talk with the children and the neighbors bringing things to eat and the big bouquet of flowers the office gang would send—the flowers that under other circumstances he never would have seen. The minister would drop in for a moment and manage to get in a quiet word or two of comfort, all the time making it seem to be no more than a friendly call. In the morning the mail would bring many little cards and notes of friendship sent by people who wanted him to know they thought of him and would have liked to have been with him if there had been the time. But they would not intrude, for the time that was left was a family time.

119

The family would sit and talk, remembering the happy days—the dog that Eddie had and the time John had run away from home for an hour or two and the first time Mary had ever had a date and the dress she wore. They'd take out the snapshot albums and look at the pictures, recalling all the days of bittersweetness and would know that theirs had been a good life—and especially he would know. And through it all would run the happy clatter of grandchildren playing in the house, climbing up on Granddad's knee to have him tell a story.

All so civilized, he thought.

Giving all of them a chance to prove they were civilized. He'd have to go back inside the house now, for he could hear Florence arranging the flowers in the birthday vase that was blue and gold. And they had so much to say to one another—even after forty years they still had so much to say to one another.

He turned and glanced back at the garden.

Most beautiful flowers, he thought, that they had ever raised.

He'd go out in the morning, when the dew was on them, when they were most beautiful, to bid them all good-by.

Green Thumb

I HAD COME BACK from lunch and was watching the office while Millie went out to get a bite to eat. With my feet up on the desk in a comfortable position, I was giving considerable attention to how I might outwit a garbage-stealing dog.

The dog and I had carried on a feud for months and I was about ready to resort to some desperate measures.

I had blocked up the can with heavy concrete blocks so he couldn't tip it over, but he was a big dog and could stand up and reach down into the can and drag all the garbage out. I had tried putting a heavy weight on the lid, but he simply dragged it off and clamly proceeded with his foraging. I had waited up and caught him red-handed at it and heaved some rocks and whatever else was handy at him, but he recognized tactics such as these for what they were and they didn't bother him. He'd come back in half an hour, calm as ever.

I had considered setting a light muskrat trap on top of the garbage so that, when he reached down into the can, he'd get his muzzle caught. But if I did that, sure as hell I'd forget to take it out some Tuesday morning and the garbageman would get caught instead. I had toyed with the idea of wiring the can so the dog would get an electric shock when he came fooling around. But I didn't know how to go about wiring it and, if I did, ten to one I'd fix it up so I'd electrocute him instead of just scaring him off, and I didn't want to kill him.

I like dogs, you understand. That doesn't mean I have

to like *all* dogs, does it? And if you had to scrape up garbage every morning, you'd be just as sore at the mutt as I was.

While I was wondering if I couldn't put something in a particularly tempting bit of garbage that would make him sick and still not kill him, the phone rang.

It was old Pete Skinner out on Acorn Ridge.

"Could you come out?" he asked.

"Maybe," I said. "What you got?"

"I got a hole out in the north forty."

"Sink-hole?"

"Nope. Looks like someone dug it out and carried off the dirt."

"Who would do that, Pete?"

"I don't know. And that ain't all of it. They left a pile of sand beside the hole."

"Maybe that's what they dug out of the hole."

"You know well enough," said Pete, "that I haven't any sandy soil. You've run tests enough on it. All of mine is clay."

"I'll be right out," I told him.

A county agent gets some funny calls, but this one topped them all. Hog cholera, corn borers, fruit blight, milk production records—any of these would have been down my alley. But a hole in the north forty?

And yet, I suppose I should have taken it as a compliment that Pete called me. When you've been a county agent for fifteen years, a lot of farmers get to trust you and some of them, like Pete, figure you can straighten out any problem. I enjoy a compliment as much as anybody. It's the headaches that go with them that I don't like.

When Millie came back, I drove out to Pete's place, which is only four or five miles out of town.

Pete's wife told me that he was up in the north forty, so I went there and found not only Pete, but some of his neighbors. All of them were looking at the hole and doing a lot of talking. I never saw a more puzzled bunch of people.

The hole was about thirty feet in diameter and about thirty-five feet deep, an almost perfect cone—not the kind of hole you'd dig with a pick and shovel. The sides were cut as clean as if they'd been machined, but the soil was not compressed, as it would have been if machinery had been used.

The pile of sand lay just a short distance from the hole. Looking at it, I had the insane feeling that, if you shoveled that sand into the hole, it would exactly fit. It was the whitest sand I've ever seen and, when I walked over to the pile and picked up some of it, I saw that it was clean. Not just ordinary clean, but *absolutely* clean—as though laundered grain by grain.

I stood around for a while, like the rest of them, staring at the hole and the pile of sand and wishing I could come up with some bright idea. But I wasn't able to. There was the hole and there was the sand. The topsoil was dry and powdery and would have shown wheelmarks or any other kind if there'd been any. There weren't.

I told Pete maybe he'd better fence in the whole business, because the sheriff or somebody from the state, or even the university, might want to look it over. Pete said that was a good idea and he'd do it right away.

I went back to the farmhouse and asked Mrs. Skinner to give me a couple of fruit jars. One of them I filled with a sample from the sand pile and the other with soil from the hole, being careful not to jolt the walls.

By this time, Pete and a couple of the neighbors had gotten a wagonload of fence posts and some wire and were coming out to the field. I waited and helped unload the posts and wire, then drove back to the office, envying Pete. He was satisfied to put up the fence and let me worry about the problem.

I found three fellows waiting for me. I gave Millie the fruit jars and asked her to send them right away to the Soils Bureau at the State Farm Campus. Then I settled down to work.

Other people drifted in and it was late in the afternoon

before I could call up the Soils Bureau and tell them I wanted the contents of the two jars analyzed. I told them a little of what had happened, although not all of it for, when you tried to put it into words, it sounded pretty weird.

"Banker Stevens called and asked if you'd drop by his place on your way home," Millie told me.

"What would Stevens want with me?" I asked. "He isn't a farmer and I don't owe him any money."

"He grows fancy flowers," said Millie.

"I know that. He lives just up the street from me."

"From what I gathered, something awful happened to them. He was all broken up."

So, on the way home, I stopped at the Stevens place. The banker was out in the yard, waiting for me. He looked terrible. He led me around to the big flower garden in the back and never have I seen such utter devastation. In that whole area, there wasn't a single plant alive. Every one of them had given up the ghost and was lying wilted on the ground.

"What could have done it, Joe?" asked Stevens and, the way he said it, I felt sorry for him.

After all, those flowers were a big thing in his life. He'd raised them from special seed and he'd babied them along, and for anybody who is crazy about flowers, I imagine they were tops.

"Someone might have used some spray on them," I said. "Almost any kind of spray, if you don't dilute it enough, would kill them."

Out in the garden, I took a close look at the dead flowers, but nowhere could I see any sign of the burning from too strong a spray.

Then I saw the holes, at first only two or three of them, then, as I went on looking, dozens of them. They were all over the garden, about an inch in diameter, for all the world as if someone had taken a broomstick and punched holes all over the place. I got down on my knees and could see that they tapered, the way they do when you pull weeds with big taproots out of the ground.

"You been pulling weeds?" I asked.

"Not big ones like that," said the banker. "I take good care of those flowers, Joe. You know that. Keep them weeded and watered and cultivated and sprayed. Put just the right amount of commercial fertilizer in the soil. Try to keep it at top fertility."

"You should use manure. It's better than all the commercial fertilizer you can buy."

"I don't agree with you. Tests have proved . . ."

It was an old argument, one that we fought out each year. I let him run on, only half listening to him, while I picked up some of the soil and crumbled it. It was dead soil. You could feel that it was. It crumbled at the lightest touch and was dry, even when I dug a foot beneath the surface.

"You water this bed recently?" I asked.

"Last evening," Stevens said.

"When did you find the flowers like this?"

"This morning. They looked fine last night. And now—" he blinked fast.

I asked him for a fruit jar and filled it with a sample of the soil.

"I'll send this in and see if there's anything wrong with it," I said.

A bunch of dogs were barking at something in the hedge in front of my place when I got home. Some of the dogs in the neighborhood are hell on cats. I parked the car and picked up an old hoe handle and went out to rescue the cat they seemed to have cornered.

They scattered when they saw me coming and I started to look in the hedge for the cat. There wasn't any and that aroused my curiosity and I wondered what the dogs could have been barking at. So I went hunting.

And I found it.

It was lying on the ground, close against the lower

growth of the hedge, as if it had crawled there for protection.

I reached in and pulled it out—a weed of some sort, about five feet tall, and with a funny root system. There were eight roots, each about an inch in diameter at the top and tapering to a quarter inch or so. They weren't all twisted up, but were sort of sprung out, so that there were four to the side, each set of four in line. I looked at their tips and I saw that the roots were not broken off, but ended in blunt, strong points.

The stalk, at the bottom, was about as thick as a man's fist. There were four main branches covered with thick, substantial, rather meaty leaves; but the last foot of the branches was bare of leaves. At the top were several flower or seed pouches, the biggest of them about the size of an old-fashioned coffee mug.

I squatted there looking at it. The more I looked, the more puzzled I became. As a county agent, you have to know quite a bit about botany and this plant was like none I had seen before.

I dragged it across the lawn to the tool shed back of the garage and tossed it in there, figuring that after supper I'd have a closer look at it.

I went in the house to get my evening meal ready and decided to broil a steak and fix up a bowl of salad.

A lot of people in town wonder at my living in the old homestead, but I'm used to the house and there seemed to be no sense in moving somewhere else when all it costs me is taxes and a little upkeep. For several years before Mother died, she had been quite feeble and I did all the cleaning and helped with the cooking, so I'm fairly handy at it.

After I washed the dishes, I read what little there was to read in the evening paper and then looked up an old text on botany, to see if I could find anything that might help identify the plant.

I didn't find anything and, just before I went to bed, I got a flashlight and went out, imagining, I suppose, that

I'd find the weed somehow different from the way I remembered it.

I opened the door of the shed and flashed the light where I'd tossed the weed on the floor. At first I couldn't see it, then I heard a leafy rustling over in one corner and I turned the light in that direction.

The weed had crawled over to one corner and it was trying to get up, its stem bowed out—the way a man would arch his back—pressing against the wall of the shed.

Standing there with my mouth open, watching it try to raise itself erect, I felt horror and fear. I reached out to the corner nearest the door and snatched up an ax.

If the plant had succeeded in getting up, I might have chopped it to bits. But, as I stood there, I saw the thing would never make it. I was not surprised when it slumped back on the floor.

What I did next was just as unreasoning and instinctive as reaching for the ax.

I found an old washtub and half filled it with water. Then I picked up the plant—it had a squirmish feel to it, like a worm—stuck its roots into the water, and pushed the tub back against the wall, so the thing could be braced upright.

I went into the house and ransacked a couple of closets until I found the sunlamp I'd bought a couple of years back, to use when I had a touch of arthritis in my shoulder. I rigged up the lamp and trained it on the plant, not too close. Then I got a big shovelful of dirt and dumped it in the tub.

And that, I figured, was about all I could do. I was giving the plant water, soil-food and simulated sunlight. I was afraid that, if I tried a more fancy treatment, I might kill it, for I hadn't any notion of what conditions it might be used to.

Apparently I handled it right. It perked up considerably and, as I moved about, the coffee-cup-sized pod on the top kept turning, following every move I made.

I watched it for a while and moved the sunlamp back

a little, so there'd be no chance of scorching it, and went back into the house.

It was then that I really began to get bone-scared. I had been frightened out in the shed, of course, but that had been shock. Now, thinking it over, I began to understand more clearly what sort of creature I'd found underneath the hedge. I remember I wasn't yet ready to say it out loud, but it seemed probable that my guest was an alien intelligence.

I did some wondering about how it had gotten here and if it had made the holes in Banker Stevens' flowerbed and also if it could have had anything to do with the big hole out in Pete Skinner's north forty.

I sat around, arguing with myself, for a man just does not go prowling around in his neighbor's garden after midnight.

But I had to know.

I walked up the alley to the back of the Stevens house and sneaked into the garden. Shielding the flashlight with my hat, I had another look at the holes in the ruined flowerbed. I wasn't too surprised when I saw that they occurred in series of eight, four to the side—exactly the kind of holes the plant back in my toolshed would make if it sank its roots into the ground.

I counted at least eleven of those eight-in-line sets of holes and I'm sure that there were more. But I didn't want to stick around too long, for fear Banker Stevens might wake up and ask questions.

So I went back home, down the alley, and was just in time to catch that garbage-stealing dog doing a good job on the can. He had his head stuck clear down into it and I was able to sneak up behind him. He heard me and struggled to get out, but he'd jammed himself into the can. Before he could get loose, I landed a good swift kick where it did maximum good. He set some kind of canine speed record in getting off the premises, I imagine.

I went to the toolshed and opened the door. The tub half full of muddy water was still there and the sunlamp was still burning—but the plant was gone. I looked all over the shed and couldn't find it. So I unplugged the sunlamp and headed for the house.

To be truthful, I was a little relieved that the plant had wandered off.

But when I rounded the corner of the house, I saw it hadn't. It was in the window box, and the geraniums I had nursed all spring were hanging limply over the side of the box.

I stood there and looked at it and had the feeling that it was looking back at me.

And I remembered that not only had it had to travel from the toolshed to the house and then climb into the window box, but it had had to open the toolshed door and close it again.

It was standing up, stiff and straight, and appeared to be in the best of health. It looked thoroughly incongruous in the window box—as if a man had grown a tall stalk of corn there, although it didn't look anything like a stalk of corn.

I got a pail of water and poured it into the window box. Then I felt something tapping me on the head and looked up. The plant had bent over and was patting me with one of its branches. The modified leaf at the end of the branch had spread itself out to do the patting and looked something like a hand.

I went into the house and up to bed and the main thing I was thinking about was that, if the plant got too troublesome or dangerous, all I had to do was mix a strong dose of commercial fertilizer or arsenic, or something just as deadly, and water it with the mixture.

Believe it or not, I went to sleep.

Next morning I got to thinking that maybe I should repair the old greenhouse and put my guest in there and be sure to keep the door locked. It seemed to be reasonably friendly and inoffensive, but I couldn't be sure, of course.

After breakfast, I went out into the yard to look for it, with the idea of locking it in the garage for the day, but it wasn't in the window box, or anywhere that I could see. And since it was Saturday, when a lot of farmers came to town, with some of them sure to be dropping in to see me, I didn't want to be late to work.

I was fairly busy during the day and didn't have much time for thinking or worrying. But when I was wrapping up the sample of soil from the banker's garden to send to the Soils Bureau, I wondered if maybe there wasn't someone at the university I should notify. I also wondered about letting someone in Washington know, except I didn't have the least idea whom to contact, or even which department.

Coming home that evening, I found the plant anchored in the garden, in a little space where the radishes and lettuce had been. The few lettuce plants still left in the ground were looking sort of limp, but everything else was all right. I took a good look at the plant. It waved a couple of its branches at me—and it wasn't the wind blowing them, for there wasn't any wind—and it nodded its coffee-cup pod as if to let me know it recognized me. But that was all it did.

After supper, I scouted the hedge in front of the house and found two more of the plants. Both of them were dead.

My next-door neighbors had gone to a movie, so I scouted their place, too, and found four more of the plants, under bushes and in corners where they had crawled away to die.

I wondered whether it might not have been the plant I'd rescued that the dogs had been barking at the night before. I felt fairly sure it was. A dog might be able to recognize an alien being where a man would be unable to.

I counted up. At least seven of the things had picked out Banker Stevens' flowerbed for a meal and the chemical fertilizer he used had killed all but one of them. The sole survivor, then, was out in the garden, killing off my lettuce.

I wondered why the lettuce and geraniums and Stevens' flowers had reacted as they did. It might be that the alien

130

plants produced some sort of poison, which they injected into the soil to discourage other plant life from crowding their feeding grounds. That was not exactly far-fetched. There are trees and plants on Earth that accomplish the same thing by various methods. Or it might be that the aliens sucked the soil so dry of moisture and plant food that the other plants simply starved to death.

I did some wondering on why they'd come to Earth at all and why some of them had stayed. If they had traveled from some other planet, they must have come in a ship, so that hole out in Pete's north forty might have been where they stopped to replenish their food supply, dumping the equivalent of garbage beside the hole.

And what about the seven I had counted?

Could they have jumped ship? Or gone on shore leave and run into trouble, the way human sailors often do?

Maybe the ship had searched for the missing members of the party, had been unable to find them, and had gone on. If that were so, then my own plant was a marooned alien. Or maybe the ship was still hunting.

I wore myself out, thinking about it, and went to bed early, but lay there tossing for a long time. Then, just as I was falling asleep, I heard the dog at the garbage can. You'd think after what had happened to him the night before, that he'd have decided to skip that particular can, but not him. He was rattling and banging it around, trying to tip it over.

I picked a skillet off the stove and opened the back door. I got a good shot at him, but missed him by a good ten feet. I was so sore that I didn't even go out to pick up the skillet, but went back to bed.

It must have been several hours later that I was brought straight up in bed by the terror-stricken yelping of a dog. I jumped out and ran to the window. It was a bright moonlit night and the dog was going down the driveway as if the devil himself were after him. Behind him sailed the plant. It had wrapped one of its branches around his tail

131

and the other three branches were really giving him a working over.

They went up the street out of sight and, for a long time after they disappeared, I could hear the dog still yelping. Within a few minutes, I saw the plant coming up the gravel, walking like a spider on its eight roots.

It turned off the driveway and planted itself beside a lilac bush and seemed to settle down for the night. I decided that if it wasn't good for anything else, the garbage can would be safe, at least. If the dog came back again, the plant would be waiting to put the bee on him.

I lay awake for a long time, wondering how the plant had known I didn't want the dog raiding the garbage. It probably had seen—if that is the proper word—me chase him out of the yard.

I went to sleep with the comfortable feeling that the plant and I had finally begun to understand each other.

The next day was Sunday and I started working on the greenhouse, putting it into shape so I could cage up the plant. It had found itself a sunny spot in the garden and was imitating a large and particularly ugly weed I'd been too lazy to pull out.

My next-door neighbor came over to offer free advice, but he kept shifting uneasily and I knew there was something on his mind.

Finally he came out with it. "Funny thing—Jenny swears she saw a big plant walking around in your yard the other day. The kid saw it, too, and he claims it chased him." He tittered a little, embarrassed. "You know how kids are."

"Sure," I said.

He stood around a while longer and gave me some more advice, then went across the yard and home.

I worried about what he had told me. If the plant really had taken to chasing kids, there'd be hell to pay.

I worked at the greenhouse all day long, but there was a lot to do, for it had been out of use ten years or more, and by nightfall I was tuckered out.

After supper, I went out on the back stoop and sat on the steps, watching the stars. It was quiet and restful.

I hadn't been there more than fifteen minutes when I heard a rustling. I looked around and there was the plant, coming up out of the garden, walking along on its roots.

It sort of squatted down beside me and the two of us just sat there, looking at the stars. Or, at least, I looked at them. I don't actually know if the plant could see. If it couldn't, it had some other faculty that was just as good as sight. We just sat there.

After a while, the plant moved one of its branches over and took hold of my arm with that handlike leaf. I tensed a bit, but its touch was gentle enough and I sat still, figuring that if the two of us were to get along, we couldn't start out by flinching away from one another.

Then, so gradually that at first I didn't notice it, I began to perceive a sense of gratitude, as if the plant might be thanking me. I looked around to see what it was doing and it wasn't doing a thing, just sitting there as I was, but with its "hand" still on my arm.

Yet in some way, the plant was trying to make me understand that it was grateful to me for saving it.

It formed no words, you understand. Other than rustling its leaves, it couldn't make a sound. But I understood that some system of communication was in operation. No words, but emotion—deep, clear, utterly sincere emotion.

It eventually got a little embarrassing, this nonstop gratitude.

"Oh, that's all right," I said, trying to put an end to it. "You would have done as much for me."

Somehow, the plant must have sensed that its thanks had been accepted, because the gratitude wore off a bit and something else took over—a sense of peace and quiet.

The plant got up and started to walk off and I called out to it, "Hey, Plant, wait a minute!"

It seemed to understand that I had called it back, for it turned around. I took it by a branch and started to lead it around the boundaries of the yard. If this communication business was going to be any good, you see, it had to go beyond the sense of gratitude and peace and quiet. So I led the plant all the way around the yard and I kept thinking at it as hard as I could, telling it not to go beyond that perimeter.

By the time I'd finished, I was wringing wet with effort. But, finally, the plant seemed to be trying to say okay. Then I built up a mental image of it chasing a kid and I shook a mental finger at it. The plant agreed. I tried to tell it not to move around the yard in daylight, when people would be able to see it. Whether the concept was harder or I was getting tired, I don't know, but both the plant and I were limp when it at last indicated that it understood.

Lying in bed that night, I thought a lot about this problem of communication. It was not telepathy, apparently, but something based on mental pictures and emotions.

But I saw it as my one chance. If I could learn to converse, no matter how, and the plant could learn to communicate something beyond abstracts to me, it could talk to people, would be acceptable and believable, and the authorities might be willing to recognize it as an intelligent being. I decided that the best thing to do would be to acquaint it with the way we humans lived and try to make it understand why we lived that way. And since I couldn't take my visitor outside the yard, I'd have to do it inside.

I went to sleep, chuckling at the idea of my house and yard being a classroom for an alien.

The next day I received a phone call from the Soils Bureau at the university.

"What kind of stuff if this you're sending us?" the man demanded.

"Just some soil I picked up," I said. "What's wrong with it?"

"Sample One is all right. It's just common, everyday Burton County soil. But Sample Two, that sand—good God, man, it has gold dust and flakes of silver and some copper in it! All of it in minute particles, of course. But if some farmer out your way has a pit of that stuff, he's rich."

"At the most, he has twenty-five or thirty truckloads of it."

"Where'd he get it? Where'd it come from?"

I took a deep breath and told him all I knew about the incident out at Pete's north forty.

He said he'd be right out, but I caught him before he hung up and asked him about the third sample.

"What was he growing on that ground?" the man asked baffledly. "Nothing I know of could suck it that clean, right down to the bare bone! Tell him to put in a lot of organic material and some lime and almost everything else that's needed in good soil, before he tries to use it."

The soils people came out to Pete's place and they brought along some other men from the university. A little later in the week, after the papers had spelled out big headlines, a couple of men from Washington showed up. But no one seemed able to figure it out and they finally gave up. The newspapers gave it a play and dropped it as soon as the experts did.

During that time, curiosity seekers flocked to the farm to gape at the hole and the pit of sand. They had carried off more than half the sand and Pete was madder than hell about the whole business.

"I'm going to fill in that hole and forget all about it," he told me, and that was what he did.

Meanwhile, at home, the situation was progressing. Plant seemed to understand what I had told him about not moving out of the yard and acting like a weed during the daytime and leaving kids alone. Everything was peaceable and I got no more complaints. Best of all, the garbage-stealing dog never showed his snout again.

Several times, during all the excitement out at Pete's place, I had been tempted to tell someone from the university about Plant. In each case, I decided not to, for we weren't getting along too well in the talk department.

But in other ways, we were doing just fine.

I let Plant watch me while I took an electric motor apart and then put it together again, but I wasn't too sure he knew what it was all about. I tried to show him the concept of mechanical power and I demonstrated how the motor would deliver that power and I tried to tell him what electricity was. But I got all bogged down with that, not knowing too much about it myself. I don't honestly think Plant got a thing out of that electric motor.

With the motor of the car, though, we were more successful. We spent one whole Sunday dismantling it and then putting it back together. Watching what I was doing, Plant seemed to take a lot of interest in it.

We had to keep the garage door locked and it was a scorcher of a day and, anyhow, I'd much rather spend a Sunday fishing than tearing down a motor. I wondered a dozen times if it was worth it, if there might not be easier ways to teach Plant the facts of our Earth culture.

I was all tired out and failed to hear the alarm and woke up an hour later than I should. I jumped into my clothes, ran out to the garage, unlocked the door and there was Plant. He had parts from that motor strewn all over the floor and he was working away at it, happy as a clam. I almost took an ax to him, but I got hold of myself in time. I locked the door behind me and walked to work.

All day, I wondered how Plant had gotten into the garage. Had he sneaked back in the night before, when I wasn't looking, or had he been able to pick the lock? I wondered, too, what sort of shape I'd find the car in when I got home. I could just see myself working half the night, putting it back together.

I left work a little early. If I had to work on the car, I wanted an early start.

When I got home, the motor was all assembled and Plant was out in the garden, acting like a weed. Seeing him there, I realized he knew how to unlock the door, for I'd locked it when I left that morning.

I turned on the ignition, making bets with myself that it wouldn't start. But it did. I rode around town a little to check it and there wasn't a thing wrong with it.

For the next lesson, I tried something simpler. I got my carpentry tools and showed them to Plant and let him watch me while I made a bird house. Not that I needed any more bird houses. The place already crawled with them. But it was the easiest, quickest thing I could think of to show Plant how we worked in wood.

He watched closely and seemed to understand what was going on, all right, but I detected a sadness in him. I put my hand on his arm to ask him what was the matter.

All that I got was a mournful reaction.

It bewildered me. Why should Plant take so much interest in monkeying around with a motor and then grieve at the making of a bird house? I didn't get it figured out until a few days later, when Plant saw me picking a bouquet of flowers for the kitchen table.

And then it hit me.

Plant was a plant and flowers were plants and so was lumber, or at least lumber at one time had been a plant. And I stood there, with the bouquet dangling in my hand and Plant looking at me, and I thought of all the shocks he had in store for him when he found out more about us —how we slaughtered our forests, grew plants for food and clothing, squeezed or boiled drugs from them.

It was just like a human going to another planet, I realized, and finding that some alien life form grew humans for food.

Plant didn't seem to be sore at me nor did he shrink from me in horror. He was just sad. When he got sad, he was the saddest-looking thing you could possibly imagine. A bloodhound with a hangover would have looked positively joyous in comparison.

If we ever had gotten to the point where we could have really talked—about things like ethics and philosophy, I mean—I might have learned just how Plant felt about our
137

plant-utilizing culture. I'm sure he tried to tell me, but I couldn't understand much of what he was driving at.

We were sitting out on the steps one night, looking at the stars. Earlier, Plant had been showing me his home planet, or it may have been some of the planets he had visited. I don't know. All I could get were fuzzy mental pictures and reactions. One place was hot and red, another blue and cold. There was another that had all the colors of the rainbow and a cool, restful feel about it, as if there might have been gentle winds and fountains and birdsongs in the twilight.

We had been sitting there for a quite a while when he put his hand back on my arm again and he showed me a plant. He must have put considerable effort into getting me to visualize it, for the image was sharp and clear. It was a scraggy, rundown plant and it looked even sadder than Plant looked when he got sad, if that is possible. When I started feeling sorry for it, he began to think of kindness and, when he thought of things like kindness and sadness and gratitude and happiness, he could really pour it on.

He had me thinking such big, kindly thoughts, I was afraid that I would burst. While I sat there, thinking that way, I saw the plant begin to perk up. It grew and flowered and was the most beautiful thing I had ever seen. It matured its seeds and dropped them. Swiftly, little plants sprang from the seeds and they were healthy and full of ginger, too.

I mulled that one over several days, suspecting I was crazy for even thinking what I did. I tried to shrug it off, but it wouldn't shrug. It gave me an idea.

The only way I could get rid of it was to try it out.

Out in back of the toolshed was the sorriest yellow rose in town. Why it clung to life, year after year, I could never figure out. It had been there ever since I was a boy. The only reason it hadn't been dug up and thrown away long ago was that no one had ever needed the ground it was rooted in.

I thought, if a plant ever needed help, that yellow rose was it.

So I sneaked out back of the toolshed, making sure that Plant didn't see me, and stood in front of that yellow rose. I began to think kindly thoughts about it, although God knows it was hard to think kindly toward such a wretched thing. I felt foolish and hoped none of the neighbors spotted me, but I kept at it. I didn't seem to accomplish much to start with, but I went back, time after time. In a week or so, I got so that I just naturally loved that yellow rose to pieces.

After four or five days, I began to see some change in it. At the end of two weeks, it had developed from a scraggy, no-account bush to one that any rose-fancier would have been proud to own. It dropped its bug-chewed leaves and grew new ones that were so shiny they looked as if they were waxed. Then it grew big flower buds and, in no time at all, was a blaze of yellow glory.

But I didn't quite believe it. In the back of my mind, I figured that Plant must have seen me doing it and helped along a bit. So I decided to test the process again where he couldn't interfere.

Millie had been trying for a couple of years to grow an African violet in a flower pot at the office. By this time, even she was willing to admit it was a losing battle. I had made a lot of jokes about the violet and, at times, Millie had been sore at me about it. Like the yellow rose, it was a hard-luck plant. The bugs ate it. Millie forgot to water it. It got knocked onto the floor. Visitors used it for an ashtray.

Naturally, I couldn't give it the close, intensive treatment I'd given the rose, but I made a point to stop for a few minutes every day beside the violet and think good things about it and, in a couple of weeks, it perked up considerably. By the end of the month, it had bloomed for the first time in its life.

Meanwhile, Plant's education continued.

At first, he'd balked at entering the house, but finally

trusted me enough to go in. He didn't spend much time there, for the house was too full of reminders that ours was a plant-utilizing culture. Furniture, clothing, cereal, paper—even the house itself—all were made of vegetation. I got an old butter tub and filled it with soil and put it in one corner of the dining room, so he could eat in the house if he wanted to, but I don't remember that he even once took a snack out of that tub.

Although I didn't admit it then, I knew that what Plant and I had tried to do had been a failure. Whether someone else might have done better, I don't know. I suspect he might have. But I didn't know how to go about getting in touch and I was afraid of being laughed at. It's a terrible thing, our human fear of ridicule.

And there was Plant to consider, too. How would he take being passed on to someone else? I'd screw up my courage to do something about it, and then Plant would come up out of the garden and sit beside me on the steps, and we'd talk—not about anything that mattered, really, but about happiness and sadness and brotherhood, and my courage would go glimmering and I'd have to start all over again.

I've since thought how much like two lost children we must have been, strange kids raised in different countries, who would have liked to play together, except neither knew the rules for the other's games or spoke the other's language.

I know . . . I know. According to common sense, you begin with mathematics. You show the alien that you know two and two are four. Then you draw the solar system and show him the sun on the diagram and then point to the sun overhead and you point to Earth on the diagram, then point to yourself. In this way, you demonstrate to him that you know about the solar system and about space and the stars and so on.

Then you hand him the paper and the pencil.

But what if he doesn't know mathematics? What if the two-plus-two-makes-four routine doesn't mean a thing to him? What if he's never seen a drawing? What if he can't draw—or see or hear or feel or think the way you do?

To deal with an alien, you've got to get down to basics. And maybe math isn't basic.

Maybe diagrams aren't.

In that case, you have to search for something that is.

Yet there must be certain universal basics.

I think I know what they are.

That, if nothing else, Plant taught me.

Happiness is basic. And sadness is basic. And gratitude, in perhaps a lesser sense. Kindness, too. And perhaps hatred —although Plant and I never dealt in that.

Maybe brotherhood. For the sake of humanity, I hope so.

But kindness and happiness and brotherhood are awkward tools to use in reaching specific understanding, although in Plant's world, they may not be.

It was getting on toward autumn and I was beginning to wonder how I'd take care of Plant during the winter months.

I could have kept him in the house, but he hated it there.

Then, one night, we were sitting on the back steps, listening to the first crickets of the season.

The ship came down without a sound. I didn't see it until it was about at treetop level. It floated down and landed between the house and toolshed.

I was startled for a moment, but not frightened, and perhaps not too surprised. In the back of my head, I'd wondered all the time, without actually knowing it, whether Plant's pals might not ultimately find him.

The ship was a shimmery sort of thing, as if it might not have been made of metal and was not really solid. I noticed that it had not really landed, but floated a foot or so above the grass.

Three other Plants stepped out and the oddest part of it was that there wasn't any door. They just came out of the ship and the ship closed behind them.

Plant took me by the arm and twitched it just a little, to

141

make me understand he wanted me to walk with him to the ship. He made little comforting thoughts to try to calm me down.

And all the time that this was going on, I could sense the talk between Plant and those other three—but just grasping the fringe of the conversation, barely knowing there was talk, not aware of what was being said.

And then, while Plant stood beside me, with his hand still on my arm, those other plants walked up. One by one, each took me by the other arm and stood facing me for a moment and told me thanks and happiness.

Plant told me the same, for the last time, and then the four of them walked toward the ship and disappeared into it. The ship left me standing there, watching it rise into the night, until I couldn't see it any longer.

I stood there for a long time, staring up into the sky, with the thanks and happiness fading and loneliness beginning to creep in.

I knew that, somewhere up there, was a larger ship, that in it were many other Plants, that one of them had lived with me for almost six months and that others of them had died in the hedges and fence corners of the neighborhood. I knew also that it had been the big ship that had scooped out the load of nutritious soil from Pete Skinner's field.

Finally I stopped looking at the sky. Over behind the toolshed I saw the whiteness of the yellow rose in bloom and once again I thought about the basics.

I wondered if happiness and kindness, perhaps even emotions that we humans do not know, might not be used on Plant's world as we use the sciences.

For the rose bush had bloomed when I thought kindly thoughts of it. And the African violet had found a new life in the kindness of a human.

Startling as it may seem, foolish as it may sound, it is not an unknown phenomenon. There are people who have the knack of getting the most out of a flowerbed or a

142

garden. And it is said of these people that they have green thumbs.

May it not be that *green thumbness* is not so much concerned with skill or how much care is taken of a plant, as with the kindliness and the interest of the person tending it?

For eons, the plant life of this planet has been taken for granted. It is simply there. By and large, plants are given little affection. They are planted or sown. They grow. In proper season, they are harvested.

I sometimes wonder if, as hunger tightens its grip upon our teeming planet, there may not be a vital need for the secret of *green thumbness*.

If kindness and sympathy can cause a plant to produce beyond its normal wont, then shouldn't we consider kindness as a tool to ward off Earth's hunger? How much more might be produced if the farmer loved his wheat?

It's silly, of course, a principle that could not gain acceptance.

And undoubtedly it would not work—not in a plant-utilizing culture.

For how could you keep on convincing a plant that you feel kindly toward it when, season after season, you prove that your only interest in it is to eat it or make it into clothing or chop it down for lumber?

I walked out back of the shed and stood beside the yellow rose, trying to find the answer. The yellow rose stirred, like a pretty woman who knows she's being admired, but no emotion came from it.

The thanks and happiness were gone. There was nothing left but the loneliness.

Damned vegetable aliens—upsetting a man so he couldn't eat his breakfast cereal in peace!

OUTSTANDING SCIENCE-FICTION FROM AVON

THE STAR DWELLERS
James Blish

F122   40¢

The inhabitants of Terra nicknamed them "Angels." They were exquisitely beautiful, these shimmering, fiery creatures, highly intelligent and playful. Yet they were awesome, too, considering that the youngest were four million years old, and the oldest probably participated in the First Cause, which had given birth to the whole universe. Young space cadet Jack Loftus was almost overwhelmed when he had to assume the responsibility of negotiating a treaty with them—a treaty which could mean the life or death of earth and mankind.

TALENTS, INC.
Murray Leinster

G1120   50¢

The ruthless Dictator of Mekin had subjugated twenty-two helpless planets. Now it was the turn of Kandar, and his terms were either unconditional surrender or total destruction. Faced with an overwhelming decision, it took guts for the military-minded Captain Bors to throw in his lot with TALENTS, INC., an untried scientific organization which swore it could do anything—up to, and including, stopping the invaders cold in their tracks. The fate of the Galaxy depended on whether or not TALENTS, INC. could keep its word.
